VIKING TALES

This edition published 2018
By Living Book Press

First published in 1902.

ISBN: 978-1-925729-16-0 (paperback)
978-1-922348-73-9 (hardcover)

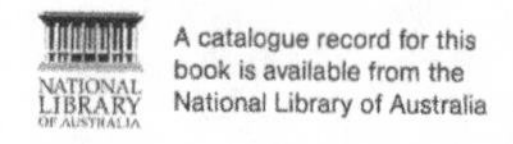

VIKING TALES
by
JENNIE HALL
The Francis W. Parker School
Chicago
ILLUSTRATED
by
VICTOR R.
LAMBDIN
LIVING BOOK
PRESS

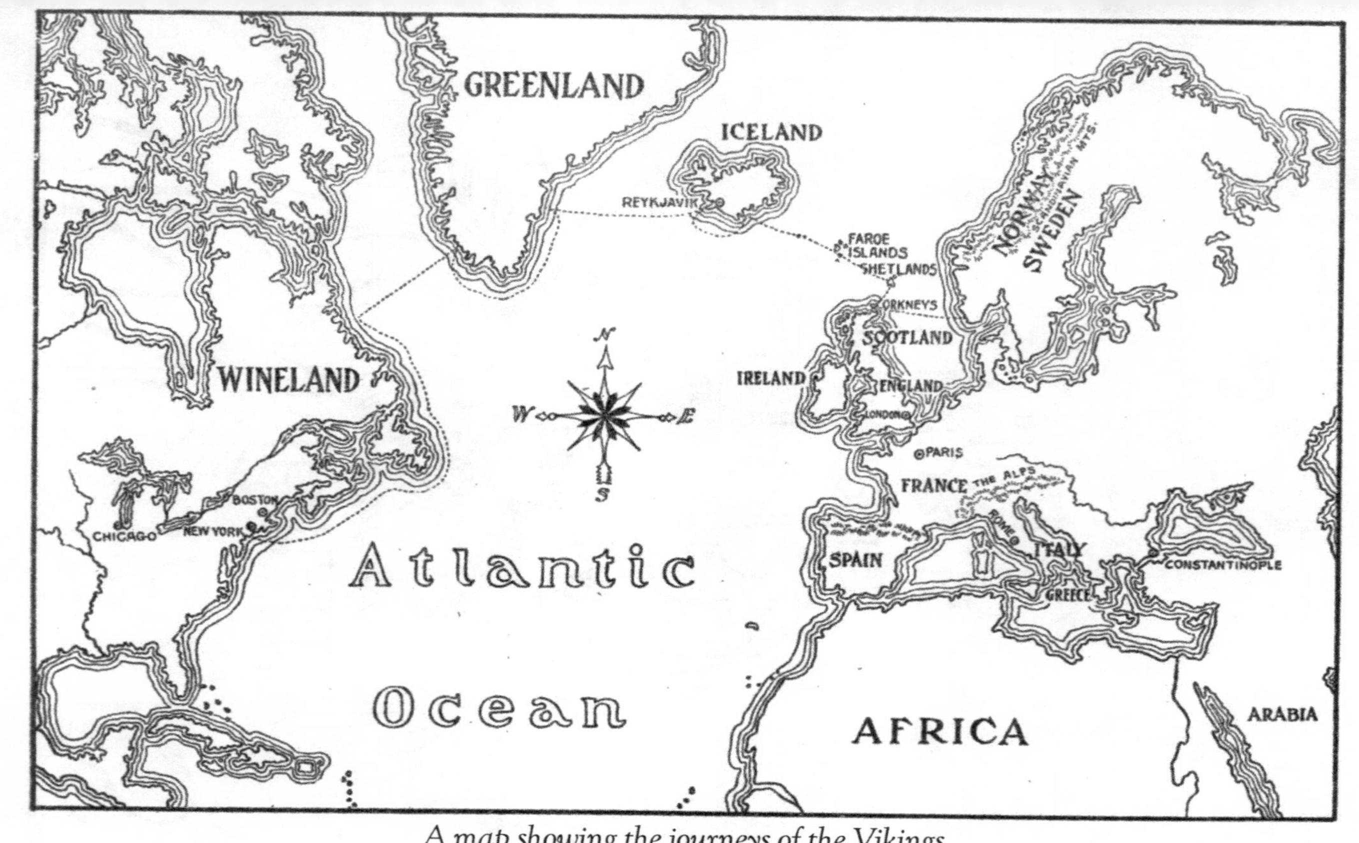

A map showing the journeys of the Vikings

The Table of Contents

ICELAND is a little country far north in the cold sea. Men found it and went there to live more than a thousand years ago. During the warm season they used to fish and make fish-oil and hunt sea-birds and gather feathers and tend their sheep and make hay. But the winters were long and dark and cold. Men and women and children stayed in the house and carded and spun and wove and knit. A whole family sat for hours around the fire in the middle of the room. That fire gave the only light. Shadows flitted in the dark corners. Smoke curled along the high beams in the ceiling. The children sat on the dirt floor close by the fire. The grown people were on a long narrow bench that they had pulled up to the light and warmth. Everybody's hands were busy with wool. The work left their minds free to think and their lips to talk, what was there to talk about? The summer's fishing, the killing of a fox, a voyage to Norway. But the people grew tired of this little gossip. Fathers looked at their children and thought:

"They are not learning much. What will make them brave and wise? What will teach them to love their country and old Norway? Will not the stories of battles, of brave deeds, of mighty men, do this?"

So, as the family worked in the red fire-light, the father told of the kings of Norway, of long voyages to strange lands, of good fights. And in farmhouses all through Iceland these old tales were told over and over until everybody knew them and loved them. Some men could sing and play the harp. This made the stories all the more interesting. People called such men "skalds," and they called their songs "sagas."

Every midsummer there was a great meeting. Men from all over Iceland came to it and made laws. During the day there were rest times, when no business was going on. Then some skald would take his harp and walk to a large stone or a knoll and stand on it and begin a song of some brave deed of an old Norse hero. At the first sound of the harp and the voice, men came running from all directions, crying out:

"The skald! The skald! A saga!"

They stood about for hours and listened. They shouted applause. When the skald was tired, some other man would come up from the crowd and sing or tell a story. As the skald stepped down from his high position, some rich man would rush up to him and say:

"Come and spend next winter at my house. Our ears are thirsty for song."

So the best skalds traveled much and visited many people. Their songs made them welcome everywhere. They were always honored with good seats at a feast. They were given many rich gifts. Even the King of Norway would sometimes send across the water to Iceland, saying to some famous skald:

"Come and visit me. You shall not go away empty-handed. Men say that the sweetest songs are in Iceland. I wish to hear them."

These tales were not written. Few men wrote or read in those days. Skalds learned songs from hearing them sung. At last people began to write more easily. Then they said:

"These stories are very precious. We must write them down to save them from being forgotten."

After that many men in Iceland spent their winters in writing books. They wrote on sheepskin; vellum, we call it. Many of these old vellum books have been saved for hundreds of years, and are now in museums in Norway. Some leaves are lost, some are torn, all are yellow and crumpled. But they are precious. They tell us all that we know about that olden time. There are the very words that the men of Iceland wrote so long ago–stories of kings and of battles and of ship-sailing. Some of those old stories I have told in this book.

PART I

IN NORWAY

The Baby

KING HALFDAN lived in Norway long ago. One morning his queen said to him:

"I had a strange dream last night. I thought that I stood in the grass before my bower.[1] I pulled a thorn from my dress. As I held it in my fingers, it grew into a tall tree. The trunk was thick and red as blood, but the lower limbs were fair and green, and the highest ones were white. I thought that the branches of this great tree spread so far that they covered all Norway and even more."

"A strange dream," said King Halfdan. "Dreams are the messengers of the gods. I wonder what they would tell us," and he stroked his beard in thought.

Some time after that a serving-woman came into the feast hall where King Halfdan was. She carried a little white bundle in her arms.

"My lord," she said, "a little son is just born to you."

"Ha!" cried the king, and he jumped up from the high seat and hastened forward until he stood before the woman.

"Show him to me!" he shouted, and there was joy in his voice.

1 See note about house on page 145.

The serving-woman put down her bundle on the ground and turned back the cloth. There was a little naked baby. The king looked at it carefully.

"It is a goodly youngster," he said, and smiled. "Bring Ivar and Thorstein."[2]

They were captains of the king's soldiers. Soon they came.

"Stand as witnesses," Halfdan said.

Then he lifted the baby in his arms, while the old serving-woman brought a silver bowl of water. The king dipped his hand into it and sprinkled the baby, saying:

"I own this baby for my son. He shall be called Harald. My naming gift to him is ten pounds of gold."

Then the woman carried the baby back to the queen's room.

"I own this baby for my son. He shall be called Harald"

"My lord owns him for his son," she said. "And no wonder! He is perfect in every limb."

The queen looked at him and smiled and remembered her dream and thought:

"That great tree! Can it be this little baby of mine?"

2 See note about names on page 145.

"I own this baby for my son. He shall be called Harald"

The Tooth Thrall

WHEN Harald was seven months old he cut his first tooth. Then his father said:

"All the young of my herds, lambs and calves and colts, that have been born since this baby was born I this day give to him. I also give to him this thrall, Olaf. These are my tooth-gifts to my son."

The boy grew fast, for as soon as he could walk about he was out of doors most of the time. He ran in the woods and climbed the hills and waded in the creek. He was much with his tooth thrall, for the king had said to Olaf:

"Be ever at his call."

Now this Olaf was full of stories, and Harald liked to hear them.

"Come out to Aegir's Rock, Olaf, and tell me stories," he said almost every day.

So they started off across the hills. The man wore a long, loose coat of white wool, belted at the waist with a strap. He had on coarse shoes and leather leggings. Around his neck was an iron collar welded together so that it could not come off. On it were strange marks, called runes, that said:

"Olaf, thrall of Halfdan."

But Harald's clothes were gay. A cape of gray

velvet hung from his shoulders. It was fastened over his breast with great gold buckles. When it waved in the wind, a scarlet lining flashed out, and the bottom of a little scarlet jacket showed. His feet and legs were covered with gray woolen tights. Gold lacings wound around his legs from his shoes to his knees. A band of gold held down his long, yellow hair.

It was a wild country that these two were walking over. They were climbing steep, rough hills. Some of them seemed made all of rock, with a little earth lying in spots. Great rocks hung out from them, with trees growing in their cracks. Some big pieces had broken off and rolled down the hill.

"Thor broke them," Olaf said. "He rides through the sky and hurls his hammer at clouds and at mountains. That makes the thunder and the lightning and cracks the hills. His hammer never misses its aim, and it always comes back to his hand and is eager to go again."

When they reached the top of the hill they looked back. Far below was a soft, green valley. In front of it the sea came up into the land and made a fiord. On each side of the fiord high walls of rock stood up and made the water black with shadow. All around the valley were high hills with dark pines on them. Far off were the mountains. In the valley were Halfdan's houses around their square yard.

"How little our houses look down there!" Harald

said. "But I can almost–yes, I can see the red dragon on the roof of the feast hall. Do you remember when I climbed up and sat on his head, Olaf?"

He laughed and kicked his heels and ran on.

At last they came to Aegir's Rock and walked up on its flat top. Harald went to the edge and looked over. A ragged wall of rock reached down, and two hundred feet below was the black water of the fiord. Olaf watched him for a while, then he said:

"No whitening of your cheek, Harald? Good! A boy that can face the fall of Aegir's Rock will not be afraid to face the war flash when he is a man."

"Ho, I am not afraid of the war flash now," cried Harald.

He threw back his cape and drew a little dagger from his belt.

"See!" he cried; "does this not flash like a sword? And I am not afraid. But after all, this is a baby thing! When I am eight years old I will have a sword, a sharp tooth of war."

He swung his dagger as though it were a long sword. Then he ran and sat on a rock by Olaf.

"Why is this Aegir's Rock?" he asked.

"You know that Asgard is up in the sky," Olaf said. "It is a wonderful city where the golden houses of the gods are in the golden grove. A high wall runs all around it. In the house of Odin, the All-father, there is a great feast hall larger than the whole earth. Its name is Valhalla. It has five hundred doors. The rafters are spears. The roof is thatched

"He threw back his cape and drew a little dagger from his belt"

with shields. Armor lies on the benches. In the high seat sits Odin, a golden helmet on his head, a spear in his hand. Two wolves lie at his feet. At his right hand and his left sit all the gods and goddesses, and around the hall sit thousands and thousands of men, all the brave ones that have ever died.

"Now it is good to be in Valhalla; for there is mead there better than men can brew, and it never runs out. And there are skalds that sing wonderful songs that men never heard. And before the doors of Valhalla is a great meadow where the warriors fight every day and get glorious and sweet wounds and give many. And all night they feast, and their wounds heal. But none may go to Valhalla except warriors that have died bravely in battle. Men who die from sickness go with women and children and cowards to Niflheim. There Hela, who is queen, always sneers at them, and a terrible cold takes hold of their bones, and they sit down and freeze.

"Years ago Aegir was a great warrior. Aegir the Big-handed, they called him. In many a battle his sword had sung, and he had sent many warriors to Valhalla. Many swords had bit into his flesh and left marks there, but never a one had struck him to death. So his hair grew white and his arms thin. There was peace in that country then, and Aegir sorrowed, saying:

"'I am old. Battles are still. Must I die in bed like a woman? Shall I not see Valhalla?'

"Now thus did Odin say long ago:

"'If a man is old and is come near death and cannot die in fight, let him find death in some brave way and he shall feast with me in Valhalla.'

"So one day Aegir came to this rock.

"'A deed to win Valhalla!' he cried.

"Then he drew his sword and flashed it over his head and held his shield high above him, and leaped out into the air and died in the water of the fiord."

"Ho!" cried Harald, jumping to his feet. "I think that Odin stood up before his high seat and welcomed that man gladly when he walked through the door of Valhalla."

"So the songs say," replied Olaf, "for skalds still sing of that deed all over Norway."

Olaf's Farm

AT another time Harald asked:

"What is your country, Olaf? Have you always been a thrall?"

The thrall's eyes flashed.

"When you are a man," he said, "and go a-viking to Denmark, ask men whether they ever heard of Olaf the Crafty. There, far off, is my country, across the water. My father was Gudbrand the Big. Two hundred warriors feasted in his hall and followed him to battle. Ten sons sat at meat with him, and I was the youngest. One day he said:

"'You are all grown to be men. There is not elbow-room here for so many chiefs. The eldest of you shall have my farm when I die. The rest of you, off a-viking!'

"He had three ships. These he gave to three of my brothers. But I stayed that spring and built me a boat. I made her for only twenty oars because I thought few men would follow me; for I was young, fifteen years old. I made her in the likeness of a dragon. At the prow I carved the head with open mouth and forked tongue thrust out. I painted the eyes red for anger.

"'There, stand so!' I said, 'and glare and hiss at

my foes.'

"In the stern I curved the tail up almost as high as the head. There I put the pilot's seat and a strong tiller for the rudder. On the breast and sides I carved the dragon's scales. Then I painted it all black and on the tip of every scale I put gold. I called her 'Waverunner.' There she sat on the rollers, as fair a ship as I ever saw.

"The night that it was finished I went to my father's feast. After the meats were eaten and the mead-horns came round, I stood up from my bench and raised my drinking-horn[3] high and spoke with a great voice:

"'This is my vow: I will sail to Norway and I will harry the coast and fill my boat with riches. Then I will get me a farm and will winter in that land. Now who will follow me?'

"'He is but a boy,' the men said. 'He has opened his mouth wider than he can do.'

"But others jumped to their feet with their mead-horns in their hands. Thirty men, one after another, raised their horns and said:

"'I will follow this lad, and I will not turn back so long as he and I live!'

"On the next morning we got into my dragon and started. I sat high in the pilot's seat. As our boat flashed down the rollers into the water I made this song and sang it:

---

3 See note about drinking-horns on page 146.

"'The dragon runs.
Where will she steer?
Where swords will sing,
Where spears will bite,
Where I shall laugh.'

"So we harried the coast of Norway. We ate at many men's tables uninvited. Many men we found overburdened with gold. Then I said:

"'My dragon's belly is never full,' and on board went the gold.

"Oh! it is better to live on the sea and let other men raise your crops and cook your meals. A house smells of smoke, a ship smells of frolic. From a house you see a sooty roof, from a ship you see Valhalla.

"Up and down the water we went to get much wealth and much frolic. After a while my men said:

"'What of the farm, Olaf?'

"'Not yet,' I answered. 'Viking is better for summer. When the ice comes, and our dragon cannot play, then we will get our farm and sit down.'

"At last the winter came, and I said to my men:

"'Now for the farm. I have my eye on one up the coast a way in King Halfdan's country.'

"So we set off for it. We landed late at night and pulled our boat up on shore and walked quietly to the house. It was rather a wealthy farm, for there were tables and a storehouse and a smithy at the sides of the house. There was but one door to the house. We went to it, and I struck it with my spear.

"I struck my shield against the door so that it made a great clanging"

"'Hello! Ho! Hello!' I shouted, and my men made a great din.

"At last some one from inside said:

"'Who calls?'

"'I call,' I answered. 'Open! or you will think it Thor who calls,' and I struck my shield against the door so that it made a great clanging.

"The door opened only a little, but I pushed it wide and leaped into the room. It was so dark that I could see nothing but a few sparks on the hearth. I stood with my back to the wall; for I wanted no sword reaching out of the dark for me.

"'Now start up the fire,' I said.

"'Come, come!' I called, when no one obeyed. 'A fire! This is cold welcome for your guests.'

"My men laughed.

"'Yes, a stingy host! He acts as though he had not expected us.'

"But now the farmer was blowing on the coals and putting on fresh wood. Soon it blazed up, and we could see about us. We were in a little feast hall,[4] with its fire down in the middle of it. There were benches for twenty men along each side. The farmer crouched by the fire, afraid to move. On a bench in a far corner were a dozen people huddled together.

"'Ho, thralls!' I called to them. 'Bring in the table. We are hungry.'

"Off they ran through a door at the back of the

---

4 See note about feast hall on page 146.

hall. My men came in and lay down by the fire and warmed themselves, but I set two of them as guards at the door.

"'Well, friend farmer,' laughed one, 'why such a long face? Do you not think we shall be merry company?'

"'We came only to cheer you,' said another. 'What man wants to spend the winter with no guests?'

"'Ah!' another then cried out, sitting up. 'Here comes something that will be a welcome guest to my stomach.'

"The thralls were bringing in a great pot of meat. They set up a crane over the fire and hung the pot upon it, and we sat and watched it boil while we joked. At last the supper began. The farmer sat gloomily on the bench and would not eat, and you cannot wonder; for he saw us putting potfuls of his good beef and basket-loads of bread into our big mouths. When the tables were taken out and the mead-horns came round, I stood up and raised my horn and said to the farmer:

"'You would not eat with us. You cannot say no to half of my ale. I drink this to your health.'

"Then I drank half of the hornful and sent the rest across the fire to the farmer. He took it and smiled, saying:

"'Since it is to my health, I will drink it. I thought that all this night's work would be my death.'

"'Oh, do not fear that,!' I laughed, 'for a dead man sets no tables.'

"So we drank and all grew merrier. At last I stood up and said:

"'I like this little taste of your hospitality, friend farmer. I have decided to accept more of it.'

"My men roared with laughter.

"'Come,' they cried, 'thank him for that, farmer. Did you ever have such a lordly guest before?'

"I went on:

"'Now there is no fun in having guests unless they keep you company and make you merry. So I will give out this law: that my men shall never leave you alone. Hakon there shall be your constant companion, friend farmer. He shall not leave you day or night, whether you are working or playing or sleeping. Leif and Grim shall be the same kind of friends to your two sons.'

"I named nine others and said:

"'And these shall follow your thralls in the same way. Now, am I not careful to make your time go merrily?'

"So I set guards over every one in that house. Not once all that winter did they stir out of sight of some of us. So no tales got out to the neighbors. Besides, it was a lonely place, and by good luck no one came that way. Oh! that was fat and easy living.

"Well, after we had been there for a long time, Hakon came in to the feast one night and said:

"'I heard a cuckoo to-day!'

"'It is the call to go a-viking,' I said.

"All my men put their hands to their mouths and

shouted. Their eyes danced. Big Thorleif stood up and stretched himself.

"'I am stiff with long sitting,' he said. 'I itch for a fight.'

"I turned to the farmer.

"'This is our last feast with you,' I said.

"'Well,' he laughed, 'this has been the busiest winter I ever spent, and the merriest. May good luck go with you!'

"'By the beard of Odin!' I cried; 'you have taken our joke like a man.'

"My men pounded the table with their fists.

"'By the hammer of Thor!' shouted Grim. 'Here is no stingy coward. He is a man fit to carry my drinking-horn, the horn of a sea-rover and a sword-swinger. Here, friend, take it,' and he thrust it into the farmer's hand. 'May you drink heart's-ease from it for may years. And with it I leave you a name. Sif the Friendly. I shall hope to drink with you sometime in Valhalla.'

"Then all my men poured around that farmer and clapped him on the shoulder and piled things upon him, saying:

"'Here is a ring for Sif the Friendly.'

"'And here is a bracelet.'

"'A sword would not be ashamed to hang at your side.'

"I took five great bracelets of gold from our treasure chest and gave them to him.

"The old man's eyes opened wide at all these

things, and at the same time he laughed.

"'May Odin send me such guests every winter!' he said.

"Early next morning we shook hands with our host and boarded the 'Waverunner' and sailed off.

"'Where shall we go?' my men asked.

"'Let the gods decide,' I said, and tossed up my spear.

"When it fell on the deck it pointed up-shore, so I steered in that direction. That is the best way to decide, for the spear will always point somewhere, and one thing is as good as another. That time it pointed us into your father's ships. They closed in battle with us and killed my men and sunk my ship and dragged me off a prisoner. They were three against one, or they might have tasted something more bitter at our hands. They took me before King Halfdan.

"'Here,' they said, 'is a rascal who has been harrying our coasts. We sunk his ship and men, but him we brought to you.'

"'A robber viking?' said the king, and scowled at me.

"I threw back my head and laughed.

"'Yes. And with all your fingers it took you a year to catch me.'

"The king frowned more angrily.

"'Saucy, too?' he said. 'Well, thieves must die. Take him out, Thorkel, and let him taste your sword.'

"Your mother, the queen, was standing by. Now

she put her hand on his arm and smiled and said:

"'He is only a lad. Let him live. And would he not be a good gift for our baby?'

"Your father thought a moment, then looked at your mother and smiled.

"'Soft heart!' he said gently to her; then to Thorkel, 'Well, let him go, Thorkel!'

"Then he turned to me again, frowning.

"'But, young sharp-tongue, now that we have caught you we will put you into a trap that you cannot get out of. Weld an iron collar on his neck.'

"So I lived and now am your tooth thrall. Well, it is the luck of war. But by the chair of Odin, I kept my vow!"

"Yes!" cried Harald, jumping to his feet. "And had a joke into the bargain. Ah! sometime I will make a brave vow like that."

Olaf's Fight With Havard

At another time Harald said:

"Tell me of a fight, Olaf. I want to hear about the music of swords."

Olaf's eyes blazed.

"I will tell you of our fight with King Havard," he said.

"One dark night we had landed at a farm. We left our 'Waverunner' in the water with three men to guard her. The rest of us went into the house. The farmer met us at the door, but he died by Thorkel's sword. The others we shut in to their beds.[5] The door at each end of the hall we had barred on the inside so that nobody could surprise us. We were busy going through the cupboards and shouting at our good luck. But suddenly we heard a shout outside:

"'Thor and Havard!'

"Then there was a great beating at the doors.

"'He has two hundred fighters with him,' said Grim; 'for we saw his ships last night. Thirty against two hundred! We shall all drink in Valhalla to-night.'

"'Well,' I cried, 'Odin shall have no unwilling guest in me.'

5 See note about beds on page 146.

"'Nor in me,' cried Hakon.

"'Nor in me,' shouted Thorkel.

"And that shout went all around, and we drew out our swords and caught up our shields.

"'Hot work is ahead of us,' said Hakon. 'Besides, we must leave none of this mead for Havard. Lend a hand some one.'

"Then he and another pulled out a great tub that sat on the floor of the cupboard.

"'I drink to Valhalla to-night.' cried Thorkel the Thirsty, and he plunged his horn deep into the tub.

"When he brought it up, his sleeve was dripping and the sweet mead was running over from the horn.

"'Sloven!' cried Hakon, and he struck Thorkel with his fist and knocked him over into the cupboard.

"He fell against the wooden wall at the back, and a carved panel swung open behind him. He dropped down head first. In a minute he put his head out of the hole again. We all stood staring.

"'I think it is a secret passage,' he said.

"'We will try it,' I answered in a whisper. 'Throw dirt on the fire. It must be dark.'

"So we dug up dirt from the earth floor and smothered the fire. All this time there was a terrible shouting and hammering at the doors, but they were of heavy logs and stood.

"'I with four more will guard this door,' I said, pointing to the east end.

"Immediately four men stepped to my side.

"'And I will guard the other,' Hakon said, and four went with him.

"'The rest of you, down the hole!' I said. 'Close the door after you. If luck is with us we will meet at the ships. Now Thor and our good swords help us! Quick! The doors are giving way.'

"So we ten men stood at the doors and held back the king's soldiers. It was dark in the room, and the people out of doors could not tell how many were inside. Few were eager to be the first in.

"'Thirty swords are waiting in there to eat up the first man,' we heard some one say.

"We chuckled at that.

"But the king stood in the very doorway and fought. Our five swords held him back for a long time, but at last he pushed in, and his men poured after him. We ran back and hid behind some tubs in a dark corner. The king's men went groping about and calling, but they did not find us. The room was full of shouting and running and sword-clashing; for in the dark and the noise the men could not tell their own soldiers. More than one fell by his friend's sword. When it was less crowded about the doorway, I whispered:

"'Follow me in double line. We will make for the ships. Keep close together.'

"So that double line of men, with swords swinging from both sides, ran out through the dark. Swords struck out at us, and we struck back. Men

"Then he turned to the shore and sang out loudly"

ran after us shouting, but our legs were as good as theirs. But I and Hakon and one other were all that reached the ship. There we saw our 'Waverunner' with sail up and bow pointing to open sea. We swam out to her and climbed aboard. Then the men swung the sail to the wind, and we moved off. Even as we went, a spear whizzed through the air, and Hakon fell dead; for the king and all his men were running to the shore.

"'After them!' they were shouting.

"Then we heard the king call, to the men in his boats lying out in the water:

"'Row to shore and take us in.'

"Thorkel was standing by my side. At that he laughed and said:

"'They do not answer. He left but a handful to guard his ships. They tasted our swords. And we went aboard and broke the oars and threw the sails into the water. It will be slow going for Havard to-night.'

"Then he turned to the shore and sang out loudly:

> "'King Havard's ships are dead:
> Olaf's dragon flies,
> King Havard stamps the shore:
> Olaf skims the waves.
> King Havard shakes his fist.
> Olaf turns and laughs.'

"That was the end of our meeting with King Havard."

Foes'-Fear

EVERY day the boy Harald heard some such story of war or of the gods, until he could see Thor riding among the storm-clouds and throwing his hammer, until he knew that a brave man has many wounds, but never a one on his back. Many nights he dreamed that he himself walked into Valhalla, and that all the heroes stood up and shouted:

"Welcome! Harald Halfdanson!"

"Ah! the bite of the sword is sweeter than the kiss of your mother," he said to Olaf one day. "When shall I stand in the prow of a dragon and feast on the fight? I am hungry to see the world. Ivar the Far-goer tells me of the strange countries he has seen. Ah! we vikings are great folk. There is no water that has not licked our boats' sides. This cape of mine came in a viking boat from France. These cloak-pins came from a far country called Greece. In my father's house are golden cups from Rome, away on the southern sea. Every land pours rich things into our treasure-chest. Ivar has been to a strange country where it is all sand and is very hot. The people call their country Arabia. They have never heard of Thor or Odin. Ivar brought beautiful striped cloth from there, and wonderful, sweet-smelling waters. Oh! when shall the white horses of the sea lead me out to strange lands and glorious battles?"

But Harald did something besides listen to stories. Every morning he was up at sunrise and went with a thrall to feed the hunting dogs. Thorstein taught him to swim in the rough waters of the fiord. Often he went with the men a-hunting in the woods and learned to ride a horse and pull a bow and throw a lance. Ivar taught him to play the harp and to make up songs. He went much to the smithy, where the warriors mended their helmets and made their spears and swords of iron and bronze. At first he only watched the men or worked the bellows, but soon he could handle the tongs and hold the red-hot iron, and after a long time he learned to use the hammer and to shape metal. One day he made himself a spear-head. It was two feet long and sharp on both edges. While the iron was hot he beat into it some runes. When the men in the smithy saw the runes they opened their eyes wide and looked at the boy, for few Norsemen could read.

"What does it say?" they asked.

"It is the name of my spear-point, and it says, 'Foes'-fear,'" Harald said. "But now for a handle."

It was winter and the snow was very deep. So Harald put on his skees and started for a wood that was back from shore. Down the mountains he went, twenty, thirty feet at a slide, leaping over chasms a hundred feet across. In his scarlet cloak he looked like a flash of fire. The wind shot past him howling. His eyes danced at the fun.

"It is like flying," he thought and laughed. "I am an eagle. Now I soar," as he leaped over a frozen river.

He saw a slender ash growing on top of a high rock.

"That is the handle for 'Foes'-fear,'" he said.

The rock stood up like a ragged tower, but he did not stop because of the steep climb. He threw off his skees and thrust his hands and feet into holes of the rock and drew himself up. He tore his jacket and cut his leather leggings and scratched his face and bruised his hands, but at last he was on the top. Soon he had chopped down the tree and had cut a straight pole ten feet long and as big around as his arm. He went down, sliding and jumping and tearing himself on the sharp stones. With a last leap he landed near his skees. As he did so a lean wolf jumped and snapped at him, snarling. Harald shouted and swung his pole. The wolf dodged, but quickly jumped again and caught the boy's arm between his sharp teeth. Harald thought of the spear-point in his belt. In a wink he had it out and was striking with it. He drove it into the wolf's neck and threw him back on the snow, dead.

"You are the first to feel the tooth of 'Foes'-fear,'"

"He drove it into the wolf's neck"

he said, "but I think you will not be the last."

Then without thinking of his torn arm he put on his skees and went leaping home. He went straight to the smithy and smoothed his pole and drove it into the haft of the spear-point. He hammered out a gold band and put it around the joining place. He made nails with beautiful heads and drove them into the pole in different places.

"If it is heavy it will strike hard," he said.

Then he weighed the spear in his hand and found the balancing point and put another gold band there to mark it.

Thorstein came in while he was working.

"A good spear," he said.

Then he saw the torn sleeve and the red wound beneath.

"Hello!" he cried. "Your first wound?"

"Oh, it is only a wolf-scratch," Harald answered.

"By Thor!" cried Thorstein, "I see that you are ready for better wounds. You bear this like a warrior."

"I think it will not be my last," Harald said.

Harald is King

NOW when Harald was ten years old his father, King Halfdan, died. An old book that tells about Harald says that then "he was the biggest of all men, the strongest, and the fairest to look upon." That about a boy ten years old! But boys grew fast in those days; for they were out of doors all the time, running, swimming, leaping on skees, and hunting in the forest. All that makes big, manly boys.

So now King Halfdan was dead and buried, and Harald was to be king. But first he must drink his father's funeral ale.

"Take down the gay tapestries that hang in the feast hall," he said to the thralls. "Put up black and gray ones. Strew the floor with pine branches. Brew twenty tubs of fresh ale and mead. Scour every dish until it shines"

Then Harald sent messengers all over that country to his kinsmen and friends.

"Bid them come in three months' time to drink my father's funeral ale," he said. "Tell them that no one shall go away empty-handed."

So in three months men came riding up at every

hour. Some came in boats. But many had ridden far through mountains, swimming rivers; for there were few roads or bridges in Norway. On account of that hard ride no women came to the feast.

At nine o'clock in the night the feast began. The men came walking in at the west end of the hall.[6] The great bonfires down the middle of the room were flashing light on everything. The clean smell of this wood-smoke and of the pine branches on the floor was pleasant to the guests. Down each side of the hall stretched long, backless benches, with room for three hundred men. In the middle of each side rose the high seat, a great carved chair on a platform. All along behind the benches were the black and gray draperies. Here hung the shields of the guests; for every man, when he was given his place, turned and hung his shield behind him and set his tall spear by it. So on each wall there was a long row of gay shields, red and green and yellow, and all shining with gold or bronze trimmings. And higher up there was another row of gleaming spear-points. Above the hall the rafters were carved and gaily painted, so that dragons seemed to be crawling across, or eagles seemed to be swooping down.

The guests walked in laughing and talking with their big voices so that the rafters rang. They made the hall look all the brighter with their clothes of scarlet and blue and green, with their flashing golden

---

6 See note about feast hall on page 146.

bracelets and head-bands and sword-scabbards, with their flying hair of red or yellow.

Across the east end of the hall was a bench. When the men were all in, the queen, Harald's mother, and the women who lived with her, walked in through the east door and sat upon this bench.

Then thralls came running in and set up the long tables[7] before the benches, Other thralls ran in with large kettles of meat. They put big pieces of this meat into platters of wood and set it before the men. They had a few dishes of silver. These they put before the guests at the middle of the tables; for the great people sat here near the high seats.

When the meat came, the talking stopped; for Norsemen ate only twice a day, and these men had had long rides and were hungry. Three or four persons ate from one platter and drank from the same big bowl of milk. They had no forks, so they ate from their fingers and threw the bones under the table among the pine branches. Sometimes they took knives from their belts to cut the meat.

When the guests sat back satisfied, Harald called to the thralls:

"Carry out the tables."

So they did and brought in two great tubs of mead and set one at each end of the hall. Then the queen stood up and called some of her women. They went to the mead tubs. They took the horns, when the thralls had filled them, and carried them

---

7 See note about tables on page 146.

to the men with some merry word. Perhaps one woman said as she handed a man his horn:

"This horn has no feet to be set down upon. You must drink it at one draught."

Perhaps another said:

"Mead loves a merry face."

The women were beautiful, moving about the hall. The queen wore a trailing dress of blue velvet with long flowing sleeves. She had a short apron of striped Arabian silk with gold fringe along the bottom. From her shoulders hung a long train of scarlet wool embroidered in gold. White linen covered her head. Her long yellow hair was pulled around at the sides and over her breast and was fastened under the belt of her apron. As she walked, her train made a pleasant rustle among the pine branches. She was tall and straight and strong, Some of her younger women wore no linen on their heads and had their white arms bare, with bracelets shining on them. They, too, were tall and strong.

All the time men were calling across the fire to one another asking news or telling jokes and laughing.

An old man, Harald's uncle, sat in the high seat on the north side. That was the place of honor. But the high seat on the south side was empty; for that was the king's seat. Harald sat on the steps before it.

The feast went merrily until long after midnight. Then the thralls took some of the guests to the guest house to sleep, and some to the beds around the sides of the feast hall. But some men lay down on the benches and drew their cloaks over themselves.

On the next night there was another feast. Still Harald sat on the step before the high seat. But when the tables were gone and the horns were going around, he stood up and raised high a horn of ale and said loudly:

"This horn of memory I drink in honor of my father, Halfdan, son of Gudrod, who sits now in Valhalla. And I vow that I will grind my father's foes under my heel."

Then he drank the ale and sat down in the king's high seat, while all the men stood and raised their horns and shouted:

"King Harald!"

And some cried:

"That was a brave vow."

And Harald's uncle called out:

"A health to King Harald!"

And they all drank it.

Then a man stood up and said:

"Hear my song of King Halfdan!" for this man was a skald.

"Yes, the song!" shouted the men, and Harald nodded his head.

So the skald took down his great harp from the wall behind him and went and stood before Harald.

"I vow that I will grind my father's foes under my heel"

The bottom of the harp rested on the floor, but the top reached as high as the skald's shoulders. The brass frame shone in the light. The strings were some of gold and some of silver. The man struck them with his hand and sang of King Halfdan, of his battles, of his strong arm and good sword, of his death, and of how men loved him.

When he had finished, King Harald took a bracelet from his arm and gave it to him, saying:

"Take this as thanks for your good song."

The guests stayed the next day and at night there was another feast. When the mead horns were going around, King Harald stood up and spoke:

"I said that no man should go away empty-handed from drinking my father's funeral ale."

He beckoned the thralls, and they brought in a great treasure-chest and set it down by the high seat. King Harald opened it and took out rich gifts–capes and sword-belts and beautiful cloth and bracelets and gold cloak-pins. These he sent about the hall and gave something to every man. The guests wondered at the richness of his gifts.

"This young king has an open hand," they said, "and deep treasure-chests."

After breakfast the next morning the guests went out and stood by their horses ready to go, but before they mounted, thralls brought a horn of mead to each man. That was called the stirrup-horn; because after they drank it the men put their feet to the stirrups and sprang upon their horses and started. King Harald and his people rode a little way with them.

All men said that that was the richest funeral feast that ever was held.

Harald's Battle

NOW King Halfdan had many foes. When he was alive they were afraid to make war upon him, for he was a mighty warrior. But when Harald became king, they said:

"He is but a lad. We will fight with him and take his land."

So they began to make ready. King Harald heard of this and he laughed and said:

"Good! 'Foes'-fear' is thirsty, and my legs are stiff with much sitting."

He called three men to him. To one he gave an arrow, saying:

"Run and carry this arrow north. Give it into the hands of the master of the next farm, and say that all men are to meet here within two weeks from this day. They must come ready for war and mounted on horses. Say also that if a man does not obey this call, or if he receives this arrow and does not carry it on to his next neighbor, he shall be outlawed from this country, and his land shall be taken from him."

He gave arrows to the other two men and told them to run south and east with the same message.

So all through King Harald's country men were

soon busy mending helmets and polishing swords and making shields. There was blazing of forges and clanging of anvils all through the land.

On the day set, the fields about King Harald's house were full of men and horses. After breakfast a horn blew. Every man snatched his weapons and jumped upon his horse. Men of the same neighborhood stood together, and their chief led them. They waited for the starting horn. This did not look like our army. There were no uniforms. Some men wore helmets, some did not. Some wore coats of mail, but others wore only their jackets and tights of bright-colored wool. But at each man's left side hung a great shield. Over his right shoulder went his sword-belt and held his long sword under his left hand. Above most men's heads shone the points of their tall spears. Some men carried axes in their belts. Some carried bows and arrows. Many had ram's horns hanging from their necks.

King Harald rode at the front of his army with his standard-bearer beside him. Chain-armor covered the king's body. A red cloak was thrown over his shoulders. On his head was a gold helmet with a dragon standing up from it. He carried a round shield on his left arm. The king had made that shield himself. It was of brass. The rivets were of silver, with strangely shaped heads. On the back of Harald's horse was a red cloth trimmed with the fur of ermine.

King Harald looked up at his standard and

laughed aloud.

"Oh, War-lover," he cried, "you and I ride out on a gay journey."

A horn blew again and the army started. The men shouted as they went, and blew their ram's horns.

"Now we shall taste something better than even King Harald's ale," shouted one.

Another rose in his stirrups and sniffed the air.

"Ah! I smell a battle," he cried. "It is sweeter than those strange waters of Arabia."

So the army went merrily through the land. They carried no tents, they had no provision wagons.

"The sky is a good enough tent for a soldier," said the Norsemen. "Why carry provisions when they lie in the farms beside you?"

After two days King Harald saw another army on the hills.

"Thorstein," he shouted," up with the white shield and go tell King Haki to choose his battle-field. We will wait but an hour. I am eager for the frolic."

So Thorstein raised a white shield on his spear as a sign that he came on an errand of peace. He rode near King Haki, but he could not wait until he came close before he shouted out his message and then turned and rode back.

"Tell your boy king that we will not hang back," Haki called after Thorstein.

King Harald's men waited on the hillside and

watched the other army across the valley. They saw King Haki point and saw twenty men ride off as he pointed. They stopped in a patch of hazel and hewed with their axes.

"They are getting the hazels," said Thorstein.

"Audun," said King Harald to a man near him, "stay close to my standard all day. You must see the best of the fight. I want to hear a song about it after it is over."

This Audun was the skald who sang at the drinking of King Halfdan's funeral ale.

King Haki's men rode down into the valley. They drove down stakes all about a great field. They tied the hazel twigs to the stakes in a string. But they left an open space toward King Harald's army and one toward King Haki's. Then a man raised a white shield and galloped toward King Harald.

"We are ready!" he shouted.

At the same time King Haki raised a red shield. King Harald's men put their shields before their mouths and shouted into them. It made a great roaring war-cry.

"Up with the war shield!" shouted King Harald. "Horns blow!"

There was a blowing of horns on both sides. The two armies galloped down into the field and ran together. The fight had begun.

All that day long swords were flashing, spears flying, men shouting, men falling from their horses, swords clashing against shields.

"Victory flashes from that dragon," Harald's men said, pointing to the king's helmet. "No one stands before it."

And, surely, before night came, King Haki fell dead under "Foes'-fear." When he fell, a great shout went up from his warriors, and they turned and fled. King Harald's men chased them far, but during the night came back to camp. Many brought swords and helmets and bracelets or silver-trimmed saddles and bridles with them.

"Here is what we got from the foe," they said.

The next morning King Harald spoke to his men:

"Let us go about and find our dead."

So they went over all the battle-field. They put every man on his shield and carried him and laid him on a hill-top. They hung his sword over his shoulder and laid his spear by his side. So they laid all the dead together there on the hill-top. Then King Harald said, looking about:

"This is a good place to lie. It looks far over the country. The sound of the sea reaches it. The wind sweeps here. It is a good grave for Norsemen and Vikings. But it is a long road and a rough road to Valhalla that these men must travel. Let the nearest kinsman of each man come and tie on his hell-shoes. Tie them fast, for they will need them much on that hard road."

So friends tied shoes on the dead men's feet. Then King Harald said:

"Now let us make the mound."

"King Haki fell dead under 'Foe's-fear'"

Every man set to work with what tools he had and heaped earth over the dead until a great mound stood up. They piled stones on the top. On one of these stones King Harald made runes telling how these men had died.

After that was done King Harald said:

"Now set up the pole, Thorstein. Let every man bring to that pole all that he took from the foe."

So they did, and there was a great hill of things around it. Harald divided it into piles.

"This pile we will give to Thor in thanks for the victory," he said. "This pile is mine because I am king. Here are the piles for the chiefs, and these things go to the other men of the army."

So every man went away from that battle richer than he was before, and Thor looked down from Valhalla upon his full temple and was pleased.

The next morning King Harald led his army back. But on the way he met other foes and had many battles and did not lose one. The kings either died in battle or ran away, and Harald had their lands.

"He has kept his vow," men said, "and ground his father's foes under his heel."

So King Harald sat in peace for a while.

Gyda's Saucy Message

NOW Harald heard men talk of Gyda, the daughter of King Eric.

"She is very beautiful," they said, "but she is very proud, too. She can both read and make runes. No other woman in the world knows so much about herbs as she does. She can cure any sickness. And she is proud of all this!"

Now when King Harald heard that, he thought to himself:

"Fair and proud. I like them both. I will have her for my wife."

So he called his uncle, Guthorm, and said:

"Take rich gifts and go to Gyda's foster-father[8] and tell him that I will marry Gyda."

So Guthorm and his men came to that house and they told the king's message to the foster-father. Gyda was standing near, weaving a rich cloak. She heard the speech. She came up and said, holding her head high and curling her lip:

"I will not waste myself on a king of so few people. Norway is a strange country. There is a little king here and a little king there–hundreds of them scattered about. Now in Denmark there

8 See note about foster-father on page 147.

is but one great king over the whole land. And it is so in Sweden. Is no one brave enough to make all of Norway his own?"

She laughed a scornful laugh and walked away. The men stood with open mouths and stared after her. Could it be that she had sent that saucy message to King Harald? They looked at her foster-father. He was chuckling in his beard and said nothing to them. They started out of the house in anger. When they were at the door, Gyda came up to them again and said:

"Give this message to your King Harald for me: I will not be his wife unless he puts all of Norway under him for my sake."

So Guthorm and his men rode homeward across the country. They did not talk. They were all thinking. At last one said:

"How shall we give this message to the king?"

"I have been thinking of that," Guthorm said; "his anger is no little thing."

It was late when they rode into the king's yard; for they had ridden slowly trying to make some plan for softening the message, but they had thought of none.

"I see light through the wind's-eyes of the feast hall," one said.

"Yes, the king keeps feast," Guthorm said. "We must give our message before all his guests."

So they went in with very heavy hearts. There sat King Harald in the high seat. The benches on

"I will not be his wife unless he puts all of Norway under him for my sake"

both sides were full of men. The tables had been taken out, and the mead-horns were going round.

"Oh, ho!" cried King Harald. "Our messengers! What news?"

Then Guthorm said:

"This Gyda is a bold and saucy girl, King Harald. My tongue refuses to give her message."

The king stamped his foot.

"Out with it!" he cried. "What does she say?"

"She says that she will not marry so little a king," Guthorm answered.

Harald jumped to his feet. His face flushed red. Guthorm stretched out his hand.

"They are not my words, O King; they are the words of a silly girl."

"Is there any more?" the king shouted. "Go on!"

"She said: 'There is one king in Denmark and one king in Sweden. Is there no man brave enough to make himself king of all Norway? Tell King Harald that I will not marry him unless he puts all of Norway under him for my sake.'"

The guests sat speechless, staring at Guthorm. All at once the king broke into a roar of laughter.

"By the hammer of Thor!" he cried, "that is a good message. I thank you, Gyda. Did you hear it, friends? King of all Norway! Why, we are all stupids. Why did we not think of that?"

Then he raised his horn high.

"Now hear my vow. I say that I will not cut my hair or comb it until I am king of all Norway. That

I will be or I will die."

Then he drank off the horn of mead, and while he drank it, all the men in the hall stood up and waved their swords and shouted and shouted. That old hall in all its two hundred years of feasts had not heard such a noise before.

"Ah, Harald!" Guthorm cried, "surely Thor in Valhalla smiled when he heard that vow."

The men sat all night talking of that wonderful vow.

On the very next day King Harald sent out his war-arrows. Soon a great army was gathered. They marched through the country north and south and east and west, burning houses and fighting battles as they went. People fled before them, some to their own kings, some inland to the deep woods and hid there. But some went to King Harald and said:

"We will be your men."

"Then take the oath, and I will be friends with you," he said.

The men took off their swords and laid them down and came one by one and knelt before the king. They put their heads between his knees and said:

"From this day, Harald Halfdanson, I am your man. I will serve you in war. For my land I will pay you taxes. I will be faithful to you as my king."

Then Harald said:

"I am your king, and I will be faithful to you."

Many kings took that oath and thousands of

common men. Of all the battles that Harald fought, he did not lose one.

Now for a long time the king's hair and beard had not been combed or cut. They stood out around his head in a great bushy mat of yellow. At a feast one day when the jokes were going round, Harald's uncle said:

"Harald, I will give you a new name. After this you shall be called Harald Shockhead. As my naming gift I give you this drinking-horn."

"It is a good name," laughed all the men.

After that all people called him Harald Shockhead.

During these wars, whenever King Harald got a country for his own, this is what he did. He said:

"All the marshland and the woodland where no people live is mine. For his farm every man shall pay me taxes."

Over every country he put some brave, wise man and called him Earl. He said to the earls:

"You shall collect the taxes and pay them to me. But some you shall keep for yourselves. You shall punish any man who steals or murders or does any wicked thing. When your people are in trouble they shall come to you, and you shall set the thing right. You must keep peace in the land. I will not have my people troubled with robber vikings."

The earls did all these things as best they could; for they were good strong men. The farmers were happy. They said:

"We can work on our farms with peace now. Before King Harald came, something was always wrong. The vikings would come and steal our gold and our grain and burn our houses, or the king would call us to war. Those little kings are always fighting. It is better under King Harald."

But the chiefs, who liked to fight and go a-viking, hated King Harald and his new ways. One of these chiefs was Solfi. He was a king's son. Harald had killed his father in battle. Solfi had been in that battle. At the end of it he fled away with two hundred men and got into ships.

"We will make that Shockhead smart," he said.

So they harried the coast of King Harald's country. They filled their ships with gold. They ate other men's meals. They burned farmhouses behind them. The people cried out to the earls for help. So the earls had out their ships all the time trying to catch Solfi, but he was too clever for them.

In the spring he went to a certain king, Audbiorn, and said to him:

"Now, there are two things that we can do. We can become this Shockhead Harald's thralls, we can kneel before him and put our heads between his knees. Or else we can fight. My father thought it better to die in battle than to be any man's thrall. How is it? Will you join with my cousin Arnvid and me against this young Shockhead?"

"Yes, I will do it," said the king.

The Sea Fight

MANY men felt as Solfi did. So when King Audbiorn and King Arnvid sent out their war arrows, a great host gathered. All men came by sea. Two hundred ships lay at anchor in the fiord, looking like strange swimming animals because of their high carved prows and bright paint. There were red and gold dragons with long necks and curved tails. Sea-horses reared out of the water. Green and gold snakes coiled up. Sea-hawks sat with spread wings ready to fly. And among all these curved necks stood up the tall, straight masts with the long yardarms swinging across them holding the looped-up sails.

When the starting horn blew, and their sails were let down, it was like the spreading of hundreds of curious flags. Some were striped black and yellow or blue and gold. Some were white with a black raven or a brown bear embroidered on them, or blue with a white sea-hawk, or black with a gold sun. Some were edged with fur. As the wind filled the gaudy sails, and the ships moved off, the men waved their hands to the women on shore and sang:

"To the sea! To the sea!
The wind in our sail,
The sea in our face,
And the smell of the fight.
After ship meets ship,
In the quarrel of swords
King Harald shall lie
In the caves under the sea
And Norsemen shall laugh."

In the prow stood men leaning forward and sniffing the salt air with joy. Some were talking of King Harald.

"Yesterday he had a hard fight," they said. "To-day he will be lying still, dressing his wounds and mending his ships. We shall take him by surprise."

They sailed near the coast. Solfi in his "Sea-hawk" was ahead leading the way. Suddenly men saw his sail veer and his oars flash out. He had quickly turned his boat and was rowing back. He came close to King Arnvid and called:

"He is there, ahead. His boats are ready in line of battle. The fox has not been asleep."

King Arnvid blew his horn. Slowly his boats came into line with his "Sea-stag" in the middle. Again he blew his horn. Cables were thrown across from one prow to the next, and all the ships were tied together so that their sides touched. Then the men set their sails again and they went past a tongue of land into a broad fiord. There lay the long line of King Harald's ships with their fierce heads grinning and mocking at the new-comers.

Back of those prows was what looked like a long wall with spots of green and red and blue and yellow and shining gold. It was the locked shields of the men in the bows, and over every shield looked fierce blue eyes. Higher up and farther back was another wall of shields; for on the half deck in the stern of every ship stood the captain with his shield-guard of a dozen men.

Arnvid's people had furled their sails and were taking down the masts, but the ships were still drifting on with the wind. The horn blew, and quickly every man sprang to his place in bow and stern. All were leaning forward with clenched teeth and widespread nostrils. They were clutching their naked swords in their hands. Their flashing eyes looked over their shields.

Soon King Arnvid's ships crashed into Harald's line, and immediately the men in the bows began to swing their swords at one another. The soldiers of the shield-guard on the high decks began to throw darts and stones and to shoot arrows into the ships opposite them.

So in every ship showers of stones and arrows were falling, and many men died under them or got broken arms or legs. Spears were hurled from deck to deck and many of them bit deep into men's bodies. In every bow men slashed with their swords at the foes in the opposite ship. Some jumped upon the gunwale to get nearer or hung from the prowhead. Some even leaped into the enemy's boat.

King Harald's ship lay prow to prow with King Arnvid's. The battle had been going on for an hour. King Harald was still in the stern on the deck. There was a dent in his helmet where a great stone had struck. There was a gash in his shoulder where a spear had cut. But he was still fighting and laughed as he worked.

"Wolf meets wolf to-day," he said. "But things are going badly in the prow," he cried. "Ivar fallen, Thorstein wounded, a dozen men lying in the bottom of the boat!"

He leaped down from the deck and ran along the gunwale, shouting as he went:

"Harald and victory!"

So he came to the bow and stood swinging his sword as fast as he breathed. Every time it hit a man of Arnvid's men. Harald's own warriors cheered, seeing him.

"Harald and victory!" they shouted, and went to work again with good heart.

Slowly King Arnvid's men fell back before Harald's biting sword. Then Harald's men threw a great hook into that boat and pulled it alongside and still pushed King Arnvid's people back.

"Come on! Follow me!" cried Harald.

Then he leaped into King Arnvid's boat, and his warriors followed him.

"He comes like a mad wolf," King Arnvid's men said, and they turned and ran back below the deck.

Then Arnvid himself leaped down and stood

"Then he leaped into King Arnvid's boat"

with his sword raised.

"Can this young Shockhead make cowards of you all?" he cried.

But Harald's sword struck him, and he fell dead. Then a big, bloody viking of King Arnvid leaped upon the edge of the ship and stood there. He held his drinking-horn and his sword high in his hands.

"Ran[9] and not you, Shockhead, shall have them and me!" he cried, and leaped laughing into the water and was drowned.

Many other warriors chose the same death on that terrible day.

All along the line of boats men fought for hours. In some places the cables had been cut, and the boats had drifted apart. Ships lay scattered about two by two, fighting. Many boats sank, many men died, some fled away in their ships, and at the end King Harald had won the battle. So he had King Arnvid's country and King Audbiorn's country. Many men took the oath and became his friends. All people were talking of his wonderful battles.

---

9 See note about Ran on page 147.

King Harald's Wedding

IT had taken King Harald ten years to fight so many battles. And all that time he had not cut his hair or combed it. Now he was feasting one day at an earl's house. Many people were there.

"How is it, friends?" Harald said "Have I kept my vow?"

His friends answered:

"You have kept your vow. There is no king but you in all Norway."

"Then I think I will cut my hair," the king laughed.

So he went and bathed and put on fresh clothes. Then the earl cut his hair and beard and combed them and put a gold band about his head. Then he looked at him and said:

"It is beautiful, smooth, and yellow."

And all people wondered at the beauty of the king's hair.

"I will give you a new name," the earl said. "You shall no longer be called Shockhead. You shall be called Harald Fairhair."

"It is a good name," everybody cried.

Then Harald said:

"But I have another thing to do now. Guthorm, you shall take the same message to Gyda that you gave ten years ago."

So Guthorm went and brought back this answer from Gyda:

"I will marry the king of all Norway."

So when the wedding time came, Harald rode across the country to the home of Gyda's father, Eric. Many men followed him. They were all richly dressed in velvet and gold.

For three nights they feasted at Eric's house. On the next night Gyda sat on the cross-bench with her women. A long veil of white linen covered her face and head and hung down to the ground. After the mead-horns had been brought in, Eric stood up from his high seat and went down and stood before King Harald.

"Will you marry Gyda now?" he asked.

Harald jumped to his feet and laughed.

"Yes," he said. "I have waited long enough."

Then he stepped down from his high seat and stood by Eric. They walked about the hall. Before them walked thralls carrying candles. Behind them walked many of King Harald's great earls. Three times they walked around the hall. The third time they stopped before the cross-bench. King Harald and Eric stepped upon the platform, where the cross-bench was.

Eric gave a holy hammer to Harald, and it was like the hammer of Thor. Harald put it upon Gyda's lap, saying:

"With this holy hammer of Thor's, I, Harald,

"I, Harald, King of Norway, take you, Gyda, for my wife"

King of Norway, take you, Gyda, for my wife."

Then he took a bunch of keys and tied it to Gyda's girdle saying:

"This is the sign that you are mistress of my house."

After that, Eric called out loudly:

"Now are Harald, King of Norway, and Gyda, daughter of Eric, man and wife."

Then thralls brought meat and drink in golden dishes. They were about to serve it to Gyda for the bride's feast, but Harald took the dish from them and said:

"No, I will serve my bride."

So he knelt and held the platter. When he did that his men shouted. Then they talked among themselves, saying:

"Surely Harald never knelt before. It is always other people who kneel to him."

When the bride had tasted the food and touched the mead-horn to her lips she stood up and walked from the hall. All her women followed her, but the men stayed and feasted long.

On the next morning at breakfast Gyda sat by Harald's side. Soon the king rose and said:

"Father-in-law, our horses stand ready in the yard. Work is waiting for me at home and on the sea. Lead out the bride."

So Eric took Gyda by the hand and led her out of the hall. Harald followed close. When they passed through the door Eric said:

"With this hand I lead my daughter out of my house and give her to you, Harald, son of Halfdan, to be your wife. May all the gods make you happy!"

Harald led his bride to the horse and lifted her up and set her behind his saddle and said:

"Now this Gyda is my wife."

Then they drank the stirrup-horn and rode off.

"Everything comes to King Harald," his men said; "wife and land and crown and victory in battle. He is a lucky man."

King Harald Goes West-Over-Seas

NOW many men hated King Harald. Many a man said:

"Why should he put himself up for king of all of us? He is no better than I am. Am I not a king's son as well as he? And are not many of us kings' sons? I will not kneel before him and promise to be his man. I will not pay him taxes. I will not have his earl sitting over me. The good old days have gone. This Norway has become a prison. I will go away and find some other place."

So hundreds of men sailed away. Some went to France and got land and lived there. Big Rolf-go-afoot and all his men sailed up the great French River and won a battle against the French king himself. There was no way to stop the flashing of his battle-axes but to give him what he wanted. So the king made Rolf a duke, gave him broad lands and gave him the king's own daughter for wife. Rolf called his country Normandy, for old Norway. He ruled it well and was a great lord, and his sons' sons after him were kings of England.

Other Norseman went to Ireland and England and Scotland. They drew up their boats on the river banks. The people ran away before them and gathered into great armies that marched back to meet the Vikings in battle. Sometimes the Norseman lost, but oftener they won, so that they got land and lived in those countries. Their houses sat in these strange lands like warriors' camps, and the Norsemen went among their new neighbors with hanging swords and spears in hand, ever ready for fight.

There are many islands north of Scotland. They are called the Orkneys and the Shetlands. They have many good harbors for ships. They are little and rocky and bare of trees. Wild sea-birds scream around them. On some of them a man can stand in the middle and see the ocean all about him. Now the Vikings sailed to these islands and were pleased.

"It is like being always in a boat," they said. "This shall be our home."

So it went until all the lands round about were covered with vikings. Norse carved and painted houses brightened the hillsides. Viking ships sailed all the seas and made harbor in every river. Norsemen's thralls plowed the soil and planted crops and herded cattle, and gold flowed into their masters' treasure-chests. Norse warriors walked up and down the land, and no man dared to say them nay.

These men did not forget Norway. In the summers they sailed back there and harried the coast. They took gold and grain and beautiful cloth back to their homes. In Norway they left burning houses and weeping women.

"In Norway they left burning houses and weeping women"

Every summer King Harald had out his ships and men and hunted these vikings. There are many little islands about Norway. They have crags and caves and deep woods. Here the vikings hid when they saw King Harald's ships coming. But Harald ran his boat into every creek and fiord and hunted in every cave and through all the woods and among the crags. He caught many men, but most of them got away and went home laughing at Harald. Then they came back the next summer and did the same deeds over again. At last King Harald said:

"There is but one thing to do. I must sail to these western islands and whip these robbers in their own homes."

So he went with a great number of ships. He found as brave men as he had brought from Norway. These vikings had brought their old courage to their new homes. King Harald's fine ships were scarred by viking stones and scorched by viking fire. The shields of Harald's warriors had dents from viking blows. Many of those men carried viking scars all their lives. And many of King Harald's warriors walked the long, hard road to Valhalla, and feasted there with some of these very vikings that had died in King Harald's battles. But after many hard fights on land and sea, after many men had died and many had fled away to other lands, King Harald won, and he made the men that were yet in the islands take the oath, and he left his earls to rule over them. Then he went back to Norway.

"He has done more than he vowed to do," people said. "He has not only whipped the vikings, but he has got a new kingdom west-over-seas."

Then they talked of that dream that his mother had.

"King Harald was that great tree," they said. "The trunk was red with the blood of his many battles, but higher up the limbs were fair and green like this good time of peace. The topmost branches were white because Harald will live to be an old man. Just as that tree spread out until all of Norway was in its shade, and even more lands, so Harald is king of all this country and of the western islands. The many branches of that tree are the many sons of Harald, who shall be earls and kings in Norway, and their sons after them, for hundreds of years."

PART II

WEST-OVER-SEAS

Homes in Iceland

MEN had been feasting in Ingolf's house. But there was no laughing and no shouting of jokes. Ingolf sat in his high seat frowning and gloomy. His head hung on his breast. He was staring into the fire. Now he raised his head and looked about the hall.

"Comrades," he said, "what shall we do? Herstein and Holmstein died by our swords. Their kinsmen hunger to kill us. Besides, when Harald hears of our deed, there will not be a safe place in Norway for us. He will never let a man fight out an honest quarrel. Where shall we go?"

A man stood up from the bench.

"We have friends in the Shetlands," he said. "Let us find homes there."

Then Leif, in the high seat opposite Ingolf, stood up.

"No, not the Shetlands, my foster-brother.[10] They are crowded already. Besides, Harald will not long keep his hands off them. Then they will be no better than Norway. England and Ireland and Scotland are old. My eyes ache for something new. What of that far island that Floki found?

10 See note about foster-brothers on page 147.

It is empty. We could choose our land from the whole country. There is good fishing. There are green valleys. And Butter Thorolf says that butter drops from every weed. There are mountains and deserts where we may find adventure. I say, let us steer for Iceland!"

When he stopped, many of the men shouted:

"Yes! Iceland!"

But an old man stood up.

"We have all laughed at that tale of Butter Thorolf's," he said. "But Floki himself said that the sea about the island is full of ice that pushes upon the land, that no ship can live in that water in the winter, that great mountains of ice cover the island. Did not all his cattle die there of hunger and cold, and did he not come back to Norway cursing Iceland?"

"Oh, Sighvat, you are old and fearful," called out Leif, and he laughed.

Then he stretched himself up and threw back his head.

"Are we afraid of ice? Have we not seen angry water before? I have been hungry, but I have never died of it. Surely if there are fish in the sea and grass in the valleys, we can live there. I should like to stand on a hill and look around on a wide land and think, 'This is all ours,' and out upon a rough sea and think, 'Far off there are our foes and they dare not come over to us.' Besides, we shall have no Shockhead Harald to lord it over us. We can come and go and feast and fight as we please. We shall be our own kings. And our ships will be always waiting to take us away, when we are weary of it. And we shall see things that other men have never seen. I am tired of the old things. Perhaps in after days men will make songs about 'those foster-brothers, Ingolf and Leif, who made a new country in a wonderful land, and whose sons and grandsons are mighty men in Iceland!'"

Ingolf leaped up from his chair.

"By the strong arm of Thor!" he cried, "I like the sound of it. Now I make my vow."

He raised his drinking-horn.

"I vow that I will find this Iceland and pass the winter there, and that if man can live upon it I will go back there and set up my home."

"And I vow that I will follow my foster-brother," cried Leif.

And many men vowed to go.

So on the next day they began to make ready a boat. They looked her over carefully and recalked every seam and freshly painted her and put into her their strongest oars and made her a new sail.

"This will be the longest voyage that she ever made," Ingolf said.

When the work was done, they put into her great stores, axes, hammers, fish-nets, cooking-kettles, kegs of ale, chests of hard bread, chests of smoked meat, brass kettles full of flour, skin bottles of water. They stowed these things away in the ends of the ship. When they were ready they put in four head of cattle.

"We shall need the milk and perhaps the meat," Ingolf said.

Many men wished to go, but Ingolf had said:

"There is little room to spare and little food and drink. I have planned for half a year. But perhaps we must be sailing longer than that. Our food may run short. We must not have extra mouths to feed. There are thirty oars in our boat. I will take only one man for every oar, and Leif and I will steer."

So they started off. Leif stood in the prow leaning forward and looking far ahead, and he sang:

"What does the swimming dragon smell?
A stormy sea, an empty land,
Hunger, darkness, giants, fire.
Leif and his sword do laugh at that."

They sailed for days and saw no land. Sometimes they passed ships and always made sure to sail close enough to hail them.

"Where are you going?" Ingolf would call.

"To Norway," would come back the answer.

"For trade or fight?" Leif would shout.

Then would ring out a great laugh from that boat and this answer:

"A shut mouth is a good friend."

So the two ships sailed on, and the men were glad to have heard a greeting and to have called one.

But at last there were the Shetlands.

"We will go in here and rest," Ingolf said.

When they rowed to shore a certain Shetland man stood there. He watched them land and looked them all over. Then he walked up to Ingolf and said:

"You look like brave men. Welcome to Shetland. You shall come to my house and rest your legs from ship-going and fill your stomachs. I hunger for news of Norway."

So they went to his house and stayed there for three days. And good it seemed to be near a fire and in a quiet bed and before a steaming platter. When they went to the shore to start off again, the Shetland man had his thralls carry a keg of ale and a great kettle of cooked meat and put them into the ship.

"Think of me when you eat this," he said.

Then the Norsemen put to sea again and sailed for a long time.

One day a terrible storm came up; the sky was black; the wind howled through the ship. Great waves leaped in the sea.

"Down with the sail and out with the oars!" Ingolf shouted.

So the men furled the sail and took down the mast and laid it along the bottom of the boat. As they worked, one man was washed overboard and drowned. The men sat down to row, but the tumbling waves tossed the boat about and poured over her and broke three of the oars. But still the men held on. They were wet to the skin and were cold, and their arms and legs ached with the hard work, and they were hungry from the long waiting, but not one face was white with fear.

"Ran, in her caves under sea, wants us for company to-night," Ingolf laughed.

So they tossed about all night, but in the morning the wind died down. Great waves still rolled, and for days the sea was rough, but they could put up the sail. Then one day Leif, as he sat in the pilot's seat, jumped to his feet and sang:

"To eyes grown tired with looking far,
All at once appeared an island,
A stretching-place for sea-legs,
A quiet bed for backs grown stiff
On rowing-bench on rolling sea.
A place to build a red fire
And thaw the blood that sea-winds froze."

But when they came near they saw no place to land. The island was like a mountain of rock standing out of the water. The sides were steep and smooth. They sailed around it, but found no place to climb up.

"There are many other islands here," said Leif. "We will try another."

So he steered to another. It, too, was a steep rock, but one side sloped down to the water and was green with grass.

"Oh, I have not seen anything so good as that green grass since I looked into my mother's face," one man said.

There was a little harbor there. The men rowed

in and quickly jumped out and put the rollers under the ship and pulled her upon shore. Then they threw themselves down on the grass and rolled and stretched their arms and shouted for joy. After that they built a fire and warmed themselves and cooked a meal and ate like wolves. They slept there that night.

In the morning before Ingolf's men started away they were standing high up on the hillside, looking about. They saw no houses on any of the islands, but they saw smoke rise from one hillside.

"Some other men, like us, weary of the sea and stopping to rest," said Ingolf.

They saw the island they had sailed around the night before.

"There can surely be nothing but bird's nests on top of that," Sighvat said.

"Look!" cried another, pointing.

Men were standing on the flat top of that island. They were letting a boat down the steep side with ropes. When it struck the water, they made a rope fast to the rock and slid down it into the ship and sailed off.

"Some robber vikings from Scotland or Ireland," laughed Leif. "It is a good hiding place for treasure."

Soon Ingolf and his men got into their ship and were off. Old Sighvat grumbled.

"Is this land not new enough and empty enough and far enough? I am tired of sea, sea, sea, and nothing else."

"We started for Iceland," said Ingolf, "and I will not stop before I come there. I have a vow. Did you make none Sighvat?"

Then they were on the water again for weeks with no sight of land.

"Oh! I would give my right hand to see a dragon pawing the water off there and to fling a word to its men," Sighvat said.

"No hope of that," replied Ingolf. "Only three dragons before ours have ever swept this water, and men are not sailing this way for pleasure or riches."

So only the desolate sea stretched around them. Sometimes it was smooth and shining under the sun. Often it was torn by winds, and a gray sky hung over it, and the men were drenched with rain. Once they ran into a fog. For three days and nights they could not see sun or stars to steer by. They forgot which way was north. When after three days the fog lifted, they found that they had been going in the wrong direction, and they had to turn around and sail all that weary way over again. But at last one afternoon they saw a white cloud resting on the water far off. As they sailed toward it, it grew into long stretches of black, hilly shore with a blue ice mountain rising from it. The sun was going down behind that mountain, and long lines of pink and of shining green, and great purple shadows streaked the blue.

"It is Iceland!" shouted the men.

"It is like Asgard the Shining," Ingolf said.

But it was still far off. Men can see a long way there because the air is so clear. So Ingolf and his people sailed on for hours and at last came into a harbor. A little green valley sloped up from it. On one side was the bright ice mountain. Back of it were bare black and red hills. In that valley Ingolf and his men drew up their boat and camped. At supper that night one of the men said:

"I almost think I never felt a fire before or had warm food in my mouth."

The men laughed.

"It is four months since we left Norway," Ingolf said. "Few men have ever been on the sea so long."

That night they put up the awning in the boat and slept under it.

After that some men went fishing every day in the rowboat that they had. And Ingolf took others, and they sailed along the shore, seeing what kind of a land this was. But winter began to come on. Then Ingolf said:

"Remember what Floki said of the ice and the rough sea in winter. Soon we cannot sail any longer. Let us choose a place to stay and build a hut there and cut hay for our cattle."

So they did. Their hut was a little mean thing of stones and turf. They kept the cattle and hay in it. Sometimes they slept there, when it was very cold. But most of the time they ate and slept by a great bonfire out of doors where it was clean. Leif said:

"I like the cold air of the sea better than the bad-smelling air of a house, even though it is warm."

Now every day Ingolf and Leif and some of the men walked about the island. At night they all sat around the campfire and talked of what they had seen during the day.

"This is surely a wonderful land," Ingolf said once. "It is at the same time like Niflheim and like Asgard. Here is a spot green and soft, a sweet cradle for men. Next it is a mountain of ice where men would freeze to death. And next to that is a hill of rock that seems to have come out of some great fire. Yesterday I saw a cave on the seashore. The door of it was big enough for a giant. The waves broke at the doorstep. A terrible roaring came from the cave. I think it is the home of a giant. I think that giants of fire and giants of frost made this island. I have seen great basins in the rocks filled with warm water. They looked like giants' bath-tubs. I have seen boiling water shoot up out of the ground. I have walked, and have felt and heard a great rumbling under me though some giant were sleeping there and turning over in his sleep. One day I stood on a mountain and looked inland. There was a wide desert of sand and black and red rock with nothing growing on it. The fierce wind blew dirt into my eyes, and the cold of it froze the marrow in my bones. When I have seen these things I have cursed the country, and have said: 'The gods hate Iceland. I will not stay here.' But then I have walked through beautiful warm valleys where the winds did not come. I saw in my mind the flowers that we found last summer. I saw our cattle feeding on the sweet grass. I thought of the sea full of good fish. I saw my house built among green fields, and my wife sitting in her home, and my children playing among the flowers and making up tales about the bright ice mountains. I saw the wide, rough seas between me and Harald and our foes. Then I thought to myself, 'It is the sweetest home on earth.' As for me, I am coming here to live. What do you say, comrades?"

"Have I not vowed to follow you, foster-brother?" said Leif. "And indeed I never saw a land that I liked better. I don't believe in your giants. My sword is my god, and my ship is my temple, and I like this land to set them up in."

They sat about the fire long that night making plans.

"You shall go home and get our women and our things, Ingolf," said Leif. "I will off to Ireland and have a frolic. There will be little play of swords in this empty land, and I want to have one last game before I hang up my battle-knife. Besides, I will come to you with a ship full of gold and clothes and house-hangings such as we cannot get here, and they will cost me nothing but the swing of a sword."

As they talked, Ingolf looked up at the sky. The northern lights were quivering there. They were like great flames of yellow and green and red.

"See," he said, and pointed. "We are not so far that the gods will forget us. There is the flash of the armor of the Valkyrias.[11] A battle is on somewhere, and Odin has sent his maidens to choose the heroes for Valhalla."

Leif only laughed and lay down to sleep.

So in the spring they all went back to Norway. Leif got ready the boat again and merrily sailed for Ireland.

"Here I go to get riches for our new land," he said.

Ingolf set his men to cutting down pines in the forest and some to building a new ship. He had his thralls plant large crops of grain and grind flour and make new kegs and chests of wood. He himself worked much at the forge, making all kinds of tools–spades, axes, hammers, hunting-knives, cooking kettles. The women were busy weaving and sewing new clothes. Ingolf sold his house and land and everything that he could not take with him.

After about two years Leif came back. He had ten thralls that he had got in Ireland. He took Ingolf aboard his ship and raised the covers of great chests. Gold helmets, silver-trimmed drinking-horns, embroidered robes, and swords flashed out.

"Did I not say that I would come back with a full ship?" he laughed.

At last all things were ready for starting.

---

11 See note about Valkyrias on page 147.

"To-day I will sacrifice to Thor and Odin," Ingolf said. "If the omens are good we will start to-morrow."

"Well, go, foster-brother," laughed Leif. "But I have better things to do. I will be putting the cattle into the ship and will have all ready."

So Ingolf and his men went into the forests a little way. There in a cleared space stood a large building. In front of this temple the men killed two horses for Odin. Ingolf caught some of the blood in a brass bowl. He raised it and looked up at the sky and said:

"All-wise and all-father Odin, and Thor who loves the thunder, I give these horses to you. Tell me whether it is your will that we go to Iceland."

As he said that, a raven flew over his head. Ingolf watched it.

"It is Odin's will that we go," he said. "He sent his raven[12] to tell us. It is flying straight toward Iceland."

The men shouted with joy at that.

Now they hung some of the meat of the horses on a tree near the temple.

"For the ravens of Odin," they said.

Ingolf carried the bowl of blood into the temple. He went through the feast hall in front to a little room at the back. Here stood wooden statues of the gods in a semicircle. Before them was a stone altar. Ingolf took a little brush of twigs that lay on

---

12 See note about Odin's ravens on page 148.

it and dipped it into the blood and sprinkled the statues.

"You shall taste of our sacrifice," he said. "Look kindly on us from your happy seats in Asgard."

Then they went into the feast hall. There thralls were boiling the horseflesh in pots over the fire. The tables were standing ready before the benches. Ingolf walked to the high seat. All the others took their places at the benches. When the horns came round, Ingolf made this vow:

"I vow that I will build my house wherever these pillars lead me."

He put his hand upon a tall post that stood beside the high seat. There was one at each side. They were the front posts of the chair. But they stood up high, almost to the roof. They were wonderfully carved and painted with men and dragons. On the top of each one was a little statue of Thor with his hammer.

At the end of the feast Ingolf had his thralls dig these pillars up. He had a little bronze chest filled with the earth that was under the altar.

"I will take the pillars of my high seat to Iceland," he said, "and I will set up my altar there upon the soil of Norway, the soil that all my ancestors have trod, the soil that Thor loves."

So they carried the pillars and the chest of earth and the statues of the gods, and put them into Ingolf's boat.

"It is a well-packed ship," the men said. 'There

is no spot to spare."

Tools, and chests of food, and tubs of drink and chests of clothes, and fishing nets were stowed in the bows of both boats. In the bottom were laid some long, heavy, hewn logs.

"The trees in Iceland are little," Ingolf said. "We must take the great beams for our homes with us."

Standing on these logs were a few cattle and sheep and horses and pigs. The rowers' benches were along the sides. In the stern of each boat was a little cabin. Here the women and children were to sleep. But the men would sleep on the timbers in the middle of the boat and perhaps they would put up the awning sometimes.

At last everyone was aboard. Men loosed the rope that held the boats. The ships flashed down the rollers into the water, and Ingolf and Leif were off for Iceland. As they sailed away everyone looked back at the shore of old Norway. There were tears in the women's eyes. Helga, Leif's wife, sang:

"There was I born. There was I wed.
There are my father's bones.
There are the hills and fields,
The streams and rocks that I love.
There are houses and temples,
Women and warriors and feasts,
Ships and songs and fights–
A crowded, joyous land.
I go to an empty land."

There was the same long voyage with storm

and fog. But at last the people saw again the white cloud and saw it growing into land and mountains. Then Ingolf took the pillars of his high seat and threw them overboard.

"Guide them to a good place, O Thor!" he cried.

The waves caught them up and rolled them about. Ingolf followed them with his ship. But soon a storm came up. The men had to take down the sails and masts, and they could do nothing with their oars. The two ships tossed about in the sea wherever the waves sent them. The pillars drifted away, and Ingolf could not see them.

"Remember your pillars, O Thor!" he cried.

Then he saw that Leif's ship was being driven far off.

"Ah, my fostor-brother," he thought, "shall I not have you to cheer me in this empty land? O Thor, let him not go down to the caves of Ran! He is too good a man for that."

On the next day the storm was not so hard, and Ingolf put in at a good harbor. A high rocky point stuck out into the sea. A broad bay with islands in the mouth was at the side. Behind the rocky point was a level green place with ice-mountains shining far back.

After a day or two Ingolf said:

"I will go look for my pillars."

So he and a few men got into the rowboat and went along the shore and into all the fiords, but they could not find the pillars. After a week they came back, and Ingolf said:

"I will build a house here to live in while I look for the posts. This way is uncomfortable for the women."

So he did. Then he set out again to look for the pillars, but he had no better luck and came back.

"I must stay at home and see to the making of hay and the drying of fish," he said. "Winter is coming on, and we must not be caught with nothing to eat."

So he stayed and worked and sent two of his thralls to look for the holy posts. They came back every week or two and always had to say that they had not found them. Midwinter was coming on.

'Ah!" said Ingolf's wife one day, "do you remember the gay feast that we had at Yule-time? All our friends were there. The house rang with song and laughter. Our tables bent with good things to eat. Walls were hung with gay draperies. The floor was clean with sweet-smelling pine-branches. Now look at this mean house; its dirt floor, its bare stone walls, its littleness, its darkness! Look at our long faces. No one here could make a song if he tried. Oh! I am sick for dear old Norway."

"It is Thor's fault," Ingolf cried. "He will not let me find his posts."

He strode our of the house and stood scowling at the gray sea.

"Ah, foster-brother!" he said. "It was never so gloomy when you were by my side. Where are you

"Then he saw Leif's ship was being driven afar off"

now? Shall I never hear your merry laugh again? That spot in my palm burns, and my heart aches to see you. That arch of sod keeps rising before my eyes. Our vows keep ringing in my ears."

At last the long, gloomy winter passed and spring came.

"Cheer up, good wife," Ingolf said. "Better days are coming now."

But that same day the thralls came back from looking for the posts.

"We have bad news," they said. "As we walked along the shore looking for the pillars we saw a man lying on the shore. We went up to him. He was dead. It was Leif. Two well-built houses stood near. We went to them. We knew from the carving on the door-posts that they were Leif's. We went in. The rooms were empty. Along the shore and in the wood back of the house we found all of his men, dead. There was no living thing about."

Ingolf said no word, but his face was white, and his mouth was set. He went into the house and got his spears and his shield and said to his men:

"Follow me."

They put provisions into the boat and pushed off and sailed until they saw Leif's houses on the shore of the harbor. There they saw Leif and the men who were his friends, dead. Their swords and spears were gone. Ingolf walked through the houses calling on Helga and on the thralls, but no one answered. The store house was empty.

The rich hangings were gone from the walls of the houses. There was nothing in the stables. The boat was gone.

Ingolf went out and stood on a high point of land that jutted out into the water. Far along the coast he saw some little islands. He turned to his men and said:

"The thralls have done it. I think we shall find them on those islands."

Then he went back to Leif and stood looking at him.

"What a shame for so brave a man to fall by the hands of thralls! But I have found that such things always happen to men who do not sacrifice to the gods. Ah, Leif! I did not think when we made those vows of foster-brotherhood that this would ever happen. But do not fear. I remember my promise. I had thought that a man's blood is precious in this empty land, but my vow is more precious."

Now they laid all those men together and tied on their hell-shoes.

"I need my sword for your sake, foster-brother. I cannot give you that. But you shall have my spears and my drinking-horn," said Ingolf. "Fore surely Odin has chosen you for Valhalla, even though you did not sacrifice. You are too good a man to go to Niflheim. You would make times merry in Valhalla."

So Ingolf put his spears and his drinking-horn by Leif. Then the men raised a great mound over all the dead. After that they went aboard their boat and sailed for the islands that Ingolf had seen. It was evening when they reached them.

"I see smoke rising from that one," Ingolf said, pointing.

He steered for it. It was a steep rock like that one in the Faroes, but they found a harbor and landed and climbed the steep hill and came out on top. They saw the ten thralls sitting about a bonfire eating. Helga and the other women from Leif's house sat near, huddled together, white and frightened. One of the thralls gave a great laugh and shouted:

"This is better than pulling Leif's plow. To-morrow we will sail for Ireland with all his wealth."

"To-morrow you will be freezing in Niflheim," cried Ingolf, and he leaped among them swinging his sword, and all his men followed him, and they killed those thralls.

Then Ingolf turned to Helga. She threw herself into his arms and wept. But after a while she told him this story:

"When springtime came, Leif thought that he would sow wheat. He had but one ox. The others had died during the winter. So he set the thralls to help pull the plow. I saw their sour looks and was afraid, but Leif only laughed:

"'What else can thralls expect?' he said. 'Never fear them, good wife.'

"Now one day soon after that the thralls came

running to the house calling out:

"'The ox is dead! The ox is dead!'

"Leif asked them about it. They said that a bear had come out of the woods and killed it, and that they had scared the beast away. They pointed out where it had gone. Then Leif called his men and said:

"'A hunt! I had not hoped for such great sport here. Ah, we will have a feast off that bear!'

"So they took their spears and went out into the woods. As soon as they were gone, the thralls came running into the house and took down all the swords and shields from the wall and ran out. In some way they met my lord and his men in the woods and killed them. Then they came back and took everything in the house and dragged us to the boat and sailed here."

"O my brother!" said Ingolf, "where is that song about 'those two foster-brothers, Ingolf and Leif, who made a new country in a wonderful land, and whose sons and grandsons are mighty men in Iceland'? But come home with me, Helga."

So they took the women and Leif's things and Leif's boat and sailed home. The next day after they came to Ingolf's house, Helga said:

"We have made your family larger, brother Ingolf. Will you not take Leif's two houses and live in them? He does not need them now. He would like you to have them."

"It would be pleasant to live there," Ingolf said.

"I thank you."

So the next day they loaded everything aboard the two ships and sailed for Leif's house. There they stayed for a year. Ingolf still sent his thralls out to look for the pillars. He was careful always to have hay, so his cattle prospered. That spring he planted wheat, but it did not grow well.

"This is sickly stuff," Ingolf said. "It takes too much time and work. It is better to save the land for hay. Perhaps we can sometime go back to Norway for flour."

At last one day the thralls came home and said:

"We have found the pillars."

Ingolf jumped to his feet. He cried out:

"You have kept me waiting three years, Thor. But as soon as my house and temple are built, I will sacrifice to you three horses as a thank-offering."

"It is a long way off, master," the thralls said, "and we have found much better places in our walks about the island."

"Thor knows best," Ingolf answered. "I will settle where he leads me."

So that summer they loaded everything into the ships again and sailed west along the coast until they came to the place where the pillars were. The land there was low and green. On both sides were low hills. A little lake glistened back from shore. In the valley were hot springs, with steam rising from them.

"It looks like smoke," the men said. "It is very

strange to see hot water and smoke come out of the ground."

In front of this green land was a good harbor with islands in it. Far over the sea toward the north shone a great ice mountain.

"I like the place," Ingolf said. "I will make this land mine."

So he built fires at the mouth of the river near there, and stood by them and called out loudly:

"I have put my fire at the mouth of these rivers. All the land that they drain is mine, and no man shall claim it but me. I will call this place Reykjavik."[13]

Then Ingolf built his feast hall. He himself carved the beams and the door-posts. Gaily painted dragons leaned out from the doors and stood up from the gables. Men and animals fought on the door-posts. For the doors he made at the forge great iron hinges. Their ends curved and spread all over the door. Near his feast hall he built a storehouse and a kitchen and a smithy and a stable and a bower for the women.

"We do not need a sleeping-house for guests," he said. "Who would be our guests?"

He roofed all his buildings with turf. It made them look like green mounds with gay carved and painted walls under them. He built also a temple, and on that was beautiful carving. In this he set up those statues that had been in his old temple.

13 See note about Reykjavik on page 148.

He put up, too, those pillars of his high seat that had been drifting about so long. Under them he laid the soil of Norway that he had brought in the little bronze chest.

"I have kept my vow, O Thor!" he cried.

Then he sacrificed three horses that he had promised to Thor. After that was over, he said:

"Here is a good field for sport. Let us have some of the old games that we used to play at home. Who will wrestle with me?"

So they wrestled there and ran races and swam in the water. The women sat and looked on.

"Oh, this is good to see!" Helga cried. "We are as gay as we used to be in old Norway."

But it was not many weeks before Ingolf said:

"I wish that I might sometime see sails in that harbor. I wish that I might think, 'Around this point of land is another farm, and across the bay is another. I can go there when I am very lonely.' I wish that I might sometime be invited to a feast. I wish that I might sometimes hear the good, clanging music of weapons at play. It is a good land, but we have lived alone for four years. I am hungry for new faces and for tidings of Norway."

One night as he and his men sat about the long fire in the feast hall, a servant threw a great piece of wood upon the fire. It was streaked with faded paint and it showed bits of carving.

"See," said Ingolf, pointing to it, "see what is left of a good ship's prow! What lands have you seen,

O dragon's head? What battles have you fought? What was your master's name? Where did the storm meet you? Perhaps he was coming to Iceland, comrades. Would it not have been pleasant to see his sail and to shake his hand and to welcome him to Iceland? But instead he is in Ran's caves, and only his broken prow has drifted here."

Now it was not many months after that when one of the men came running into the feast hall, shouting:

"A sail! A sail in the harbor!"

All those men gave a shout with no word in it, as though their hearts had leaped into their throats. They jumped up and ran to the shore and stood there with hungry eyes. When the men landed, those Icelanders clapped them on the shoulders, and tears ran down their faces. For a long time they could say nothing but "Welcome! Welcome!"

But after a while Ingolf led them to the feast hall and had a feast spread at once. While the thralls were at work, the men stood together and talked. Such a noise had never been in that hall before.

"We have already built our fires and claimed our land up the shore a way," the leader said. "Men in Norway talk much of Ingolf and Leif, and wonder what has happened to them."

Then Ingolf told them of all that had come to pass in Iceland, and then he asked of Norway.

"Ah! things are going from bad to worse," the newcomers said. "Harald grows mightier every

"Those Icelanders clapped them on the shoulders"

day. A man dare not swing a sword now except for the king. We came here to get away from him. Many men are talking of Iceland. Soon the sea-road between here and Norway will be swarming with dragons."

And so it was. Ships also came from Ireland and from the Shetlands and the Orkneys.

"Harald has come west-over-seas," the men of these ships said, "and has laid his heavy hand upon the islands and put his earls over them. They are no place now for free men."

So by the time Ingolf was an old man, Iceland was no longer an empty land. Every valley was spotted with bright feast halls and temples. Horses and cattle pastured on the hillsides. Smoke curled up from kitchens and smithies. Gay ships sailed the waters, taking Iceland cloth and wool and Iceland fish and oil and the soft feathers of Iceland birds to Norway to sell, and bringing back wood and flour and grain.

When Ingolf died, his men drew up on the shore the boat in which he had come to Iceland. They painted it freshly and put new gold on it, so that it stood there a glittering dragon with head raised high, looking over the water. Old Sighvat lifted a huge stone and carried it to the ship's side. With all his strength he threw it into the bottom. The timbers cracked.

"If this ship moves from here," he said, "then I do not know how to moor a ship. It is Ingolf's grave."

Then men laid Ingolf upon his shield and carried him and placed him on the high deck in the stern near the pilot's seat where he had sat to steer to Iceland. They hung his sword over his shoulder. They laid his spear by his side. In his hand they put his mead-horn. Into the ship they set a great treasure-chest filled with beautiful clothes and bracelets and head-bands. Beside the treasure-chest they piled up many swords and spears and shields. They put gold-trimmed saddles and bridles upon three horses. Then they killed the horses and dragged them into the ship. They killed hunting-dogs and put them by the horses; for they said:

"All these things Ingolf will need in Valhalla. When he walks through the door of that feast hall, Odin must know that a rich and brave man comes. When he fights with those heroes during the day, he must have weapons worthy of him. He must have dogs for the hunt. When he feasts with those heroes at night he must wear rich clothes, so that those feasters shall know that he was a wealthy man and generous, and that his friends loved him."

Ingolf's son tied on his hell-shoes for the long journey.

"If these shoes come untied," he said, "I do not know how to fasten hell-shoes."

Then he went out of the ship and stood on the ground with his family. All the men of Iceland were there.

"This is a glorious sight," they said. "Surely no

ship ever carried a richer load. Inside and out the boat blazes with gold and bronze, and, high over his riches, lies the great Ingolf, ready to take the tiller and guide to Valhalla, where all the heroes will rise up and shout him welcome."

Then the thralls heaped a mound of earth over the ship. This hill stood up against the sky and seemed to say: "Here lies a great man." Sighvat put a stone on the top, with runes on it telling whose grave it was. All this time a skald stood by and played on his harp and sang a song about that time when Ingolf came to Iceland. He called him the father of Iceland. People of that country still read an old story that the men of that long ago time wrote about Ingolf, and they love him because he was a brave man and "the first of men to come to Iceland."

Eric the Red

IT was a spring day many years after Ingolf died. All the freemen in the west of Iceland had come to a meeting. Here they made laws and punished men for having done wrong. The meeting was over now. Men were walking about the plain and talking. Everybody seemed much excited. Voices were loud, arms were swinging.

"It was an unjust decision," some one cried. "Eric killed the men in fair fight. The judges outlawed him because they were afraid. His foe Thorgest has many rich and powerful men to back him."

"No, no!" said another. "Eric is a bloody man. I am glad he is out of Iceland."

Just then a big man with bushy red hair and beard stalked through the crowd. He looked straight ahead and scowled.

"There he goes," people said, and turned to look after him.

"His hands are as red as his beard," some said, and frowned.

But others looked at him and smiled saying:

"He walks like Thor the Fearless."

"His story would make a fine song," one said. "As strong and as brave and as red as Thor! Always in a quarrel. A man of many places–Norway, the north of Iceland, the west of Iceland, those little islands off the shore of Iceland. Outlawed from all of them on account of his quarrels. Where will he go now, I wonder?"

This Eric strode down to the shore with his men following.

"He is in a black temper," they said. "We should best not talk to him."

So they made ready the boat in silence. Eric got into the pilot's seat and they sailed off. Soon they pulled the ship up on their own shore. Eric strolled into his house and called for supper. When the drinking-horns had been filled and emptied, Eric pulled himself up and smiled and shouted out so that the great room was full of his big voice:

"There is no friend like mead. It always cheers a man's heart."

Then laughter and talking began in the hall because Eric's good temper had come back. After a while Eric said:

"Well, I must off somewhere. I have been driven about from place to place, like a seabird in a storm. And there is always a storm about me. It is my sword's fault. She is ever itching to break her peace-bands[14] and be out and at the play. She has shut Norway to me and now Iceland. Where will you go next, old comrade?" and he pulled out his sword and looked at it and smiled as the fire

14 See note about peace-bands on page 148.

"He looked straight ahead of him and scowled"

"More than half the men in the hall jumped to their feet"

flashed on it.

"There are some of us who will follow you wherever you go, Eric," called a man from across the fire.

"Is it so?" Eric cried, leaping up. "Oh! then we shall have some merry times yet. Who will go with me?"

More than half the men in the hall jumped to their feet and waved their drinking-horns and shouted:

"I! I!"

Eric sat down in his chair and laughed.

"O you bloody birds of battle!" he cried. "Ever hungry for new frolic! Our swords are sisters in blood, and we are brothers in adventure. Do you know what is in my heart to do?"

He jumped to his feet, and his face glowed. Then he laughed as he looked at his men.

"I see the answer flashing from your eyes," he said, "that you will do it even if it is to go down to Niflheim and drag up Hela, the pale queen of the stiff dead."

His men pounded on the tables and shouted:

"Yes! Yes! Anywhere behind Eric!"

"But it is not to Niflheim," Eric laughed. "Did you ever hear that story that Gunnbiorn told? He was sailing for Iceland, but the fog came down, and then the wind caught him and blew him far off. While he drifted about he saw a strange land that rose up white and shining out of a blue sea. Huge ships of ice sailed out from it and met him.

I mean to sail to that land."

A great shout went up that shook the rafters. Then the men sat and talked over plans. While they sat, a stranger came into the hall.

"I have no time to drink," he said. "I have a message from your friend Eyjolf. He says that Thorgest with all his men means to come here and catch you tonight. Eyjolf bids you come to him, and he will hide you until you are ready to start; for he loves you."

"Hunted like a wolf from corner to corner of the world!" Eric cried angrily. "Will they not even let me finish one feast?"

Then he laughed.

"But if I take my sport like a wolf, I must be hunted like one. So we shall sleep to-night in the woods about Eyjolf's house, comrades, instead of in these good beds. Well, we have done it before."

"And it is no bad place," cried some of the men.

"I always liked the stars better than a smoky house fire," said one.

"Can no bad fortune spoil your good nature?" Eric laughed. "But now we are off. Let every man carry what he can."

So they quickly loaded themselves with clothes and gold and swords and spears and kettles of food. Eric led his wife Thorhild and his two young sons, Thorstein and Leif. All together they got into the boat and went to Eyjolf's farm. For a week or more they stayed in his woods, sometimes in a secret cave of his when they knew that Thorgest was about. And sometimes Eyjolf sent and said:

"Thorgest is off. Come to my house for a feast."

All this time they were making ready for the voyage, repairing the ship and filling it with stores. Word of what Eric meant to do got out, and men laughed and said:

"Is that not like Eric? What will he not do?"

Some men liked the sound of it, and they came to Eric and said:

"We will go with you to this strange land."

So all were ready and they pushed off with Eric's family aboard and those friends who had joined him. They took horses and cattle with them, and all kinds of tools and food.

"I do not well know where this land is," Eric said. "Gunnbiorn said only that he sailed east when he came home to Iceland. So I will steer straight west. We shall surely find something. I do not know, either, how long we must go."

So they sailed that strange ocean, never dreaming what might be ahead of them. They found no islands to rest on. They met heavy fogs.

One day Eric sat in the pilot's seat, he said:

"I think that I see one of Gunnbiorn's ships of ice. Shall we sail up to her and see what kind of craft she is?"

"Yes," shouted his men.

So they went on toward it.

"It sends out a cold breath," said one of the men.

They all wrapped their cloaks about them.

"It is a bigger boat than I ever saw before," said Eric. "The white mast stands as high as a hill."

"It must be giants that sail in it, frost giants," said another of the men.

But as they came nearer, Eric all at once laughed loudly and called out:

"By Thor, that Gunnbiorn was a foolish fellow. Why, look! It is only a piece of floating ice such as we sometimes see from Iceland. It is no ship, and there is no one on it."

His men laughed and one called to another and said:

"And you thought of frost giants!"

Then they sailed on for days and days. They met many of these icebergs. On one of them was a white bear.

"Yonder is a strange pilot," Eric laughed.

"I have seen bears come floating so to the north shore of Iceland," an old man said. "Perhaps they come from the land that we are going to find."

One day Eric said:

"I see afar off an iceberg larger than any one yet. Perhaps that is our white land."

But even as he said it he felt his boat swing under his hand as he held the tiller. He bore hard on the rudder, but he could not turn the ship.

"What is this?" he cried. "A strong river is running here. It is carrying our ship away from this land. I cannot make head against it. Out with the

"It is a bigger boat than I ever saw before"

oars!"

So with oars and sail and rudder they fought against the current, but it took the boat along like a chip, and after a while they put up their oars and drifted.

"Luck has taken us into its own hands," Eric laughed. "But this is as good a way as another."

Sometimes they were near enough to see the land, then they were carried out into the sea and thought that they should never see any land again.

"Perhaps this river will carry us to a whirlpool and suck us under," the men said.

But at last Eric felt the current less strong under his hand.

"To the oars again!" he called.

So they fought with the current and sailed out of it and went on toward land. But when they reached the shore they found no place to go in. Steep black walls shot up from the sea. Nothing grew on them. When the men looked above the cliffs they saw a long line of white cutting the sky.

"It is a land of ice," they said.

They sailed on south, all the time looking for a place to go ashore.

"I am sick of this endless sea," Thorhild complained, "but this land is worse."

After a while they began to see small bays cut into the shore with little flat patches of green at their sides. They landed in these places and stretched and warmed themselves and ate.

"But these spots are only big enough for graves," the men said. "We can not live here."

So they went on again. All the time the weather was growing colder. Eric's people kept themselves wrapped in their cloaks and put scarfs around their heads.

"And it is still summer!" Thorhild said. "What will it be in winter?"

"We must find a place to build a house now before the winter comes on," said Eric. "We must not freeze here."

So they chose a little spot with hills about it to keep off the wind. They made a house out of stones; for there were many in that place. They lived there that winter. The sea for a long way out from shore froze so that it looked like white land. The men went out upon it to hunt white bear and seal. They ate the meat and wore the skins to keep them warm. The hardest thing was to get fuel for the fire. No trees grew there. The men found a little driftwood along the shore, but it was not enough. So they burned the bones and the fat of the animals they killed.

"It is a sickening smell," Thorhild said. "I have not been out of this mean house for weeks. I am tired of the darkness and the smoke and the cattle. And all the time I hear great noises, as though some giant were breaking this land into pieces."

"Ah, cheer up, good wife!" Eric laughed. "I smell better luck ahead."

Once Eric and his men climbed the cliffs and went back into the middle of the land. When they came home they had this to tell:

"It is a country of ice, shining white. Nothing grows on it but a few mosses. Far off it looks flat, but when you walk upon it, there are great holes and cracks. We could see nothing beyond. There seems to be only a fringe of land around the edge of an island of ice."

The winter nights were very long. Sometimes the sun showed for an hour, sometimes for only a few minutes, sometimes it did not show at all for a week. The men hunted by the bright shining of the moon or by the northern lights.

As it grew warmer the ice in the sea began to crack and move and melt and float away. Eric waited only until there was a clear passage in the water. Then he launched his boat, and they sailed southward again. At last they found a place that Eric liked.

"Here I will build my house," he said.

So they did and lived there that summer and pastured their cattle and cut hay for the winter and fished and hunted.

The next spring Eric said:

"The land stretches far north. I am hungry to know what is there."

Then they all got into the boat again and sailed north.

"We can leave no one here," Eric had said. "We

cannot tell what might come between us. Perhaps giants or dragons or strange men might come out of this inland ice and kill our people. We must stay together."

Farther north they found only the same bare, frozen country. So after a while they sailed back to their home and lived there.

One spring after they had been in that land for four years, Eric said:

"My eyes are hungry for the sight of men and green fields again. My stomach is sick of seal and whale and bear. My throat is dry for mead. This is a bare and cold and hungry land. I will visit my friends in Iceland."

"And our swords are rusty with long resting," said his men. "Perhaps we can find play for them in Iceland."

"Now I have a plan," Eric suddenly said. "Would it not be pleasant to see other feast halls as we sail along the coast?"

"Oh! it would be a beautiful sight," his men said.

"Well," said Eric, "I am going to try to bring back some neighbors from Iceland. Now we must have a name for our land. How does Greenland sound?"

His men laughed and said:

"It is a very white Greenland, but men will like the sound of it. It is better than Iceland."

So Eric and all his people sailed back and spent the winter with his friends.

"Ah! Eric, it is good to hear your laugh again,"

they said.

Eric was at many feasts and saw many men, and he talked much of his Greenland.

"The sea is full of whale and seals and great fish," he said. "The land has bear and reindeer. There are no men there. Come back with me and choose your land."

Many men said that they would do it. Some men went because they thought it would be a great frolic to go to a new country. Some went because they were poor in Iceland and thought:

"I can be no worse off in Greenland, and perhaps I shall grow rich there."

And some went because they loved Eric and wanted to be his neighbors.

So the next summer thirty-five ships full of men and women and goods followed Eric for Greenland. But they met heavy storms, and some ships were wrecked, and the men drowned. Other men grew heartsick at the terrible storm and the long voyage and no sight of land, and they turned back to Iceland. So of those thirty-five ships only fifteen got to Greenland.

"Only the bravest and the luckiest men come here," Eric said. "We shall have good neighbors."

Soon other houses were built along the fiords.

"It is pleasant to sail along the coast now," said Eric. "I see smoke rising from houses and ships standing on the shore and friendly hands waving."

Leif and His New Land

NOW Eric had lived in Greenland for fifteen years. His sons Thorstein and Leif had grown up to be big, strong men. One spring Leif said to his father:

"I have never seen Norway, our mother land. I long to go there and meet the great men and see the places that skalds sing about."

Eric answered:

"It is right that you should go. No man has really lived until he has seen Norway."

So he helped Leif fit out a boat and sent him off. Leif sailed for months. He passed Iceland and the Faroes and the Shetlands. He stopped at all of these places and feasted his mind on the new things. And everywhere men received him gladly; for he was handsome and wise. But at last he came near Norway. Then he stood up before the pilot's seat and sang loudly:

> "My eyes can see her at last,
> The mother of mighty men,
> The field of famous fights.
> In the sky above I see
> Fair Asgard's shining roofs,
> The flying hair of Thor,

The wings of Odin's birds,
The road that heroes tread.
I am here in the land of the gods,
The land of mighty men."

For a while he walked the land as though he were in a dream. He looked at this and that and everything and loved them all because it was Norway.

"I will go to the king," he said.

He had never seen a king. There were no kings in Iceland or in Greenland. So he went to the city where the king had his fine house. The king's name was Olaf. He was a great-grandson of Harald Hairfair; for Harald had been dead a hundred years.

Now the king was going to hold a feast at night, and Leif put on his most beautiful clothes to go to it. He put on long tights of blue wool and a short jacket of blue velvet. He belted his jacket with a gold girdle. He had shoes of scarlet with golden clasps. He threw around himself a cape of scarlet velvet lined with seal fur. His long sword stuck out from under his cloak. On his head he put a knitted cap of bright colors. Then he walked to the king's feast hall and went through the door. It was a great hall, and it was full of richly-dressed men. The fires shone on so many golden head-bands and bracelets and so many glittering swords and spears on the wall, and there was so much noise of talking and laughing, that at first Leif did not know what to do. But at last he went and sat on the very end seat of the bench near him.

As the feast went on, King Olaf sat in his high seat and looked about the hall and noticed this one and that one and spoke across the fire to many. He was keen-eyed and soon saw Leif in his far seat.

"Yonder is some man of mark," he said to himself. "He is surely worth knowing. His face is not the face of a fool. He carries his head like a lord of men."

He sent a thrall and asked Leif to come to him. So Leif walked down the long hall and stood before the king.

"I am glad to have you for a guest," the king said. "What are your name and country?"

"I am Leif Ericsson, and I have come all the way from Greenland to see you and old Norway."

"From Greenland!" said the king. "It is not often that I see a Greenlander. Many come to Norway to trade, but they seldom come to the king's hall. I shall be glad to hear about your land. Come up and speak with me."

So Leif went up the steps of the high seat and sat down by the king and talked with him. When the feast was over the king said:

"You shall live at my court this winter, Leif Ericsson. You are a welcome guest."

So Leif stayed there that winter. When he started back in the spring, the king gave him two thralls as a parting gift.

"Let this gift show my love, Leif Ericsson," he said. "For your sake I shall not forget Greenland."

Leif sailed back again and had good luck until he was past Iceland. Then great winds came out of the north and tossed his ship about so that the men could do nothing. They were blown south for days and days. They did not know where they were. Then they saw land, and Leif said:

"Surely luck has brought us also to a new country. We will go in and see what kind of a place it is."

So he steered for it. As they came near, the men said:

"See the great trees and the soft, green shore. Surely this is a better country than Greenland or than Iceland either."

When they landed they threw themselves upon the ground.

"I never lay on a bed so soft as this grass," one said.

"Taller trees do not grow in Norway," said another.

"There is no stone here as in Norway, but only good black dirt," Leif said. "I never saw so fertile a land before."

The men were hungry and set about building a fire.

"There is no lack of fuel here," they said.

They stayed many days in this country and walked about to see what was there. A German, named Tyrker, was with Leif. He was a little man with a high forehead and a short nose. His eyes were big and rolling. He had lived with Eric for many years, and had taken care of Leif when he was a little boy. So Leif loved him.

Now one day they had been wandering about and all came back to camp at night except Tyrker. When Leif looked around on his comrades, he said:

"Where is Tyrker?"

No one knew. Then Leif was angry.

"Is a man of so little value in this empty land that you would lose one?" he said. "Why did you not keep together? Did you not see that he was gone? Why did you not set out to look for him? Who knows what terrible thing may have happened to him in these great forests?"

Then he turned and started out to hunt for him. His men followed, silent and ashamed. They had not gone far when they saw Tyrker running toward them. He was laughing and talking to himself. Leif ran to him and put his arms around him with gladness at seeing him.

"Why are you so late?" he asked. "Where have you been?"

But Tyrker, still smiling and nodding his head, answered in German. He pointed to the woods and laughed and rolled his eyes. Again Leif asked his question and put his hand on Tyrker's shoulder as though he would shake him. Then Tyrker answered in the language of Iceland:

"I have not been so very far, but I have found something wonderful."

"What is it?" cried the men.

"He pointed to the woods and laughed and rolled his eyes"

"I have found grapes growing wild," answered Tyrker, and he laughed, and his eyes shone.

"It cannot be," Leif said.

Grapes do not grow in Greenland nor in Iceland nor even in Norway. So it seemed a wonderful thing to these Norsemen.

"Can I not tell grapes when I see them?" cried Tyrker. "Did I not grow up in Germany, where every hillside is covered with grapevines? Ah! it seems like my old home."

"It is wonderful," Leif said. "I have heard travelers tell of seeing grapes growing, but I myself never saw it. You shall take us to them early in the morning, Tyrker."

So in the morning they went back into the woods and saw the grapes. They ate of them.

"They are like food and drink," they cried.

That day Leif said:

"We spent most of the summer on the ocean. Winter will soon be coming on and the sea about Greenland will be frozen. We must start back. I mean to take some of the things of this land to show to our people at home. We will fill the rowboat with grapes and tow it behind us. The ship we will load with logs from these great trees. That will be a welcome shipload in Greenland, where we have neither trees nor vines. Now half of you shall gather grapes for the next few days, and the other half shall cut timber."

So they did, and after a week sailed off. The ship

was full of lumber, and they towed the rowboat loaded with grapes. As they looked back at the shore, Leif said:

"I will call this country Wineland for the grapes that grow there."

One of the men leaped upon the gunwale and leaned out, clinging to the sail, and sang:

"Wineland the good, Wineland the warm,
Wineland the green, the great, the fat.
Our dragon fed and crawls away
With belly stuffed and lazy feet.
How long her purple, trailing tail!
She fed and grew to twice her size."

Then all the men waved their hands to the shore and gave a great shout for that good land.

For all that voyage they had fair weather and sailed into Eric's harbor before the winter came. Eric saw the ship and ran down to the shore. He took Leif into his arms and said:

"Oh, my son, my old eyes ached to see you. I hunger to hear of all that you have seen and done."

"Luck has followed me all the way," said Leif. "See what I have brought home."

The Greenlanders looked.

"Lumber! lumber!" they cried. "Oh! it is better stuff than gold."

Then they saw the grapes and tasted them.

"Surely you must have plundered Asgard," they said, smacking their lips.

At the feast that night Eric said:

"Leif shall sit in the place of honor."

So Leif sat in the high seat opposite Eric. All men thought him a handsome and wise man. He told them of the storm and of Wineland.

"No man would ever need a cloak there. The soil is richer than the soil of Norway. Grain grows wild, and you yourselves saw the grapes that we got from there. The forests are without end. The sea is full of fish."

The Greenlanders listened with open mouths to all this. They turned and talked to Leif's ship-comrades who were scattered among them.

Leif noticed two strangers, an old man who sat at Eric's side and a young woman on the cross-bench. He turned to his brother Thorstein who sat next to him.

"Who are these strangers?" he asked.

"Thorbiorn and his daughter Gudrid," Thorstein answered. "They landed here this spring. I never saw our father more glad of anything than to see this Thorbiorn. They were friends before we left Iceland. When they saw each other again they could not talk enough of old times. In the spring Eric means to give him a farm up the fiord a way. It seems that this Thorbiorn comes of a good family that has been rich and great in Iceland for years. And Thorbiorn himself was rich when our father knew him, and was much honored by all men. But ill luck came, and he grew poor. This hurt his pride. 'I will not stay in Iceland and be a beggar,' he said to himself. 'I will not have men look at me and say, "He is not what his father was." I will go to my friend Eric the Red in Greenland.'

"Then he got ready a great feast and invited all his friends. It was such a feast as had not been in Iceland for years. Thorbiorn spent on it all the wealth that he had left. For he said to himself, 'I will not leave in shame. Men shall remember my last feast.' After that he set out and came to Greenland.

"Is not Gudrid beautiful? And she is wise. I mean to marry her, if her father will permit it."

Now Leif settled down in Greenland and became a great man there. He was so busy and he grew so rich that he did not think of going to Wineland again. But people could not forget his story. Many nights as men sat about the long fires they talked of that wonderful land and wished to see it.

Wineland the Good

ON an autumn, a year or two after Leif came home, Eric and his men saw two large ships come to land not far down the shore from the house.

"They look like trading ships," Eric said. "Let us go down to see them."

"I will go, too," Gudrid said. "Perhaps they will have rich cloth and jewelry. It is long since I had my eyes on a new dress."

So they all went down and found two large trading ships lying in the water. A great many men were on the shore making a fire.

"Welcome to Greenland!" called Eric. "What are your names and your country?"

Then a fine, big man walked out from among the men and went up to Eric.

"I am Thorfinn," he said, "a trader. I sailed this summer from Iceland with forty men and a ship-load of goods. On the sea I met this other ship from Iceland. The master is Biarni. Come and look at my goods."

So he rowed Eric and Gudrid out and they went aboard his boat. Thorfinn opened his chests and showed Eric gleaming swords and bracelets and axes and farm tools. But before Gudrid he spread beautiful cloth and gold embroidery and golden necklaces. As they looked, he told of doings in Iceland and asked of Greenland.

"We never see such things as these in this bare land," Gudrid said, as she smoothed a beautiful dress of purple velvet. "I envy the women of Iceland their fair clothes."

"There is no need of that," Thorfinn said, "for this dress is yours and anything else from my chests that you like. Here is a necklace that I beg you to take. It did not have a fairer mistress in Greece where I got it."

"You are a very generous trader," Gudrid said.

Then Thorfinn gave Eric a great sword with a gold-studded scabbard. After a while he took them to Biarni's ship. He also gave them gifts. They all talked and laughed much while they were together.

"You are merry comrades," Eric said. "I ask you both and all your men to spend the winter at my house. You can put your goods into my storehouses."

"By my sword! a generous offer," said Thorfinn. "As for me, I am happy to come."

Biarni and all the rest said the same thing. Thorfinn walked to the house with Eric and Gudrid, while the other men sailed to the ship-sheds and pulled their boats under them.

Then Thorfinn saw to the unloading and storing of his goods.

"Is this Gudrid your daughter?" he asked of Eric

one day.

"She is the widow of my son Thorstein," Eric said. "He died the same winter that they were married. Her father, too, died not long ago. So Gudrid lives with me."

Now all that winter until Yuletime Eric spread a good feast every night. There was laughter through his house all the time. Often at the feasts the men cast lots to see whether they might sit on the cross-bench with the women. Sometimes it was Thorfinn's luck to sit by Gudrid. Then they talked gaily and drank together.

At last Yule was coming near. Eric went about the house gloomy then. One day Thorfinn put his hand on Eric's shoulder and said:

"Something is troubling you, Eric. We have all noticed that you are not gay as you used to be. Tell me what is the matter."

"You have carried yourselves like noble men in my house," Eric answered. "I am proud to have you for guests. Now I am ashamed that you should not find a house worthy of you. I am ashamed that when you leave me you will have to say that you never spent a worse Yule than you did with Eric the Red in Greenland. For my cupboards are empty."

"Oh, that is easily mended," Thorfinn said. "No house could feed eighty men so long and not feel it. I never knew so generous a host before. But I have flour and grain and mead in my boat. You are welcome to all of it. You have only to open the doors of your own storehouses. It is a little gift."

So Eric used those things, and there was never a merrier Yule feast than in his house that winter.

When Yule was over, Thorfinn said to Eric:

"Gudrid is a beautiful and wise woman. I wish to have her for my wife."

"You seem to be a man worthy of her," Eric said.

So that winter Gudrid and Thorfinn were married and lived at Eric's house.

One day Thorfinn said to Eric:

"I have heard much of this wonderful Wineland since I have been here. It seems to me that it is worth while to go and see more of it."

"My son Thorstein and I tried it once," said Eric. "It was the year after Leif came back. We set out with a fair ship and with glad hearts, but we tossed about all summer on the sea and got nowhere. We were wet with storm, lean with hunger and illness, and heartsick at our bad luck."

"And yet," Thorfinn said, "another time we might have better weather. I have never seen so fair a land as this seems to be."

Then he went to Leif and talked long with him. Leif told him in what direction he had sailed to come home, and how the shores looked that he had passed.

"I think I could find my way," Thorfinn said. "My heart moves me to try this frolic."

He spoke to Gudrid about it.

"Oh, yes!" she cried. "Let us go. It is long since

I felt a boat leaping under me. I am tired of sitting still. I want to feel the warm days and see the soft grass and the high trees and taste the grapes of this Wineland the Good."

Then he talked with his men and with Biarni.

"We are ready," they all said. "We are only waiting for a leader."

"Then let us go!" cried Thorfinn.

So in the spring they fitted up their two ships and put into them provisions and a few cattle. Some of Eric's men also got ready a boat, so that three ships set sail from Eric's harbor carrying one hundred and sixty men to Wineland. As they started, Gudrid stood on the deck and sang:

> "I will feast my eyes on new things–
> On mighty trees and purple grapes,
> On beds of flowers and soft grass.
> I will sun myself in a warm land."

They sailed on and past those shores that Leif had spoken of. Whenever they saw any interesting place they sailed in and looked about and rested there.

They had gone far south, past many fair shores with woods on them, when Gudrid said one day:

"This is a beautiful bay with a smooth green field by it, and the great mountains far back. I should like to stay there for a little while."

So they sailed in and drew their ships up on shore. They put up the awnings in them.

"These shall be our houses," Thorfinn said.

They were strange-looking houses–shining dragons with gay backs lying on the yellow sand. Near them the Norsemen lighted fires and cooked their supper. That night they slept in the ships. In the morning Gudrid said:

"I long to see what is back of that mountain."

So they all climbed it. When they stood on the top they could see far over the country.

"There is a lake that we must see," Thorfinn said.

"I should like to sail around that bay," said Biarni, pointing.

"I am going to walk up that valley yonder," one of the men said.

And everyone saw some place where he would like to go. So for all that summer they camped in that spot and went about the country seeing new things. They hunted in the woods and caught rabbits and birds and sometimes bears and deer. Every day some men rowed out to sea and fished. There was an island in the bay where thousands of birds had their nests. The men gathered eggs here.

"We have more to eat than we had in Greenland or Iceland," Thorfinn said, "and need not work at all. It is all play."

Near the end of summer Thorfinn spoke to his comrades.

"Have we not seen everything here? Let us go to a new place. We have not yet found grapes."

Thorfinn and Biarni and all their men sailed south again. But some of Eric's men went off in their boat another way. Years afterward the Greenlanders heard that they were shipwrecked and made slaves in Ireland.

After Thorfinn and Biarni had sailed for many days they landed on a low, green place. There were hills around it. A little lake was there.

"What is growing on those hillsides?" Thorfinn said, shading his eyes with his hand.

He and some others ran up there. The people on shore heard them shout. Soon they came running back with their hands full of something.

"Grapes! Grapes!" they were shouting.

All those people sat down and ate the grapes and then went to the hillside and picked more.

"Now we are indeed in Wineland," they said. "It is as wonderful as Leif's stories. Surely we must stay here for a long time."

The very next day they went into the woods and began to cut out lumber. The huts that they built were little things. They had no windows, and in the doorways the men hung their cloaks instead of doors.

"We can be out in the air so much in this warm country," said Gudrid, "that we do not need fine houses."

The huts were scattered all about, some on the side of the lake, some at the shore of the harbor, some on the hillside. Gudrid had said:

"I want to live by the lake where I can look into the green woods and hear sweet bird-noises."

So Thorfinn built his hut there.

As they sat about the campfire one night, Biarni said:

"It is strange that so good a land should be empty. I suppose that these are the first houses that were ever built in Wineland. It is wonderful to think that we are alone here in this great land."

All that winter no snow fell. The cattle pastured on the grass.

"To think of the cold, frozen winters in Greenland!" Gudrid said. "Oh! this is the sun's own land."

In the beginning of that winter a little son was born to Gudrid and Thorfinn.

"A health to the first Winelander!" the men shouted and drank down their wine; for they had made some from Wineland grapes.

"Will he be the father of a great country, as Ingolf was?" Biarni mused.

Gudrid looked at her baby and smiled.

"You will be as sunny as this good land, I hope," she said.

They named him Snorri. He grew fast and soon crept along the yellow sand, and toddled among the grapevines, and climbed into the boats and learned to talk. The men called him the "Wineland king."

"I never knew a baby before," one of the men said.

"No," said another. "Swords are jealous. But when they are in their scabbards, we can do other things, even play with babies."

"I wonder whether I have forgotten how to swing my sword in this quiet land," another man said.

One spring morning when the men got up and went out from their huts to the fires to cook they saw a great many canoes in the harbor. Men were in them paddling toward shore.

"What is this?" cried the Norsemen to one another. "Where did they come from? Are they foes? Who ever saw such boats before? The men's faces are brown."

"Let every man have his sword ready," cried Thorfinn. "But do not draw until I command. Let us go to meet them."

So they went and stood on the shore. Soon the men from the canoes landed and stood looking at the Norsemen. The strangers' skin was brown. Their faces were broad. Their hair was black. Their bodies were short. They wore leather clothes. One man among them seemed to be chief. He spread out his open hands to the Norsemen.

"He is showing us that he has no weapons," Biarni said. "He comes in peace."

Then Thorfinn showed his empty hands and asked: "What do you want?"

The stranger said something, but the Norsemen could not understand. It was some new language. Then the chief pointed to one of the huts and walked toward it. He and his men walked all around and felt of the timber and went into it and looked at all the things there–spades and cloaks and drinking-

"The chief held them out to Thorfinn and hugged the cloak to him"

horns. As they looked they talked together. They went to all the other huts and looked at everything there. One of them found a red cloak. He spread it out and showed it to the others. They all stood about it and looked at it and felt of it and talked fast.

"They seem to like my cloak," Biarni said.

One of the strangers went down to their canoes and soon came back with an armload of furs–fox-skins, otter-skins, beaver-skins. The chief took some and held them out to Thorfinn and hugged the cloak to him.

"He wants to trade," Thorfinn said. "Will you do it, Biarni?"

"Yes," Biarni answered, and took the furs.

"If they want red stuff, I have a whole roll of red cloth that I will trade," one of the other men said.

He went and got it. When the strangers saw it they quickly held out more furs and seemed eager to trade. So Thorfinn cut the cloth into pieces and sold every scrap. When the strangers got it they tied it about their heads and seemed much pleased.

While this trading was going on and everybody was good-natured, a bull of Thorfinn's ran out of the woods bellowing and came towards the crowd. When the strangers heard it and saw it they threw down whatever was in their hands and ran to their canoes and paddled off as fast as they could.

The Norsemen laughed.

"We have lost our customers," Biarni said.

"Did they never see a bull before?" laughed one of the men.

Now after three weeks the Norsemen saw canoes in the bay again. This time it was black with them, there were so many. The people in them were all making a horrible shout.

"It is a war-cry," Thorfinn said, and he raised a red shield. "They are surely twenty to our one, but we must fight. Stand in close line and give them a taste of your swords."

Even as he spoke a great shower of stones fell upon them. Some of the Norsemen were hit on the head and knocked down. Biarni got a broken arm. Still the storm came fast. The strangers had landed and were running toward the Norsemen. They threw their stones with sling-shots, and they yelled all the time.

"Oh, this is no kind of fighting for brave men!" Thorfinn cried angrily.

The Norsemen's swords swung fast, and many of the strangers died under them them, but still others came on, throwing stones and swinging stone axes. The horrible yelling and the strange things that the savages did frightened the Norsemen.

"These are not men," some one cried. Then those Norsemen who had never been afraid of anything turned and ran. But when they came to the top of a rough hill Thorfinn cried:

"What are we doing? Shall we die here in this empty land with no one to bury us? We are leaving our women."

Then one of the women ran out of the hut where

they were hiding.

"Give me a sword!" she cried. "I can drive them back. Are Norsemen not better than these savages?"

Then those warriors stopped, ashamed, and stood up before the wild men and fought so fiercely that the strangers turned and fled down to their canoes and paddled away.

"Oh, I am glad they are gone!" Thorfinn said. "It was an ugly fight."

"Thor would not have loved that battle," one said.

"It was no battle," another replied. "It was like fighting against an army of poisonous flies."

The Norsemen were all worn and bleeding and sore. They went to their huts and dressed their wounds, and the women helped them. At supper that night they talked about the fight for a long time.

"I will not stay here," Gudrid said. "Perhaps these wild men have gone away to get more people and will come back and kill us. Oh! they are ugly."

"Perhaps brown faces are looking at us now from behind the trees in the woods back there," said Biarni.

It was the wish of all to go home. So after a few days they sailed back to Greenland with good weather all the way. The people at Eric's house were very glad to see them.

"We were afraid you had died," they said.

"And I thought once that we should never leave Wineland alive," Thorfinn answered.

Then they told all the story.

"I wonder why I had no such bad luck," Leif said. "But you have a better shipload than I got."

He was looking at the bundles of furs and the kegs of wine.

"Yes "said Thorfinn, "we have come back richer than when we left. But I will never go again for all the skins in the woods."

The next summer Thorfinn took Gudrid and Snorri and all his people and sailed back to Iceland, his home. There he lived until he died. People looked at him in wonder.

"That is the man who went to Wineland and fought with wild men,'' they said. "Snorri is his son. He is the first and last Winelander, for no one will ever go there again. It will be an empty and forgotten land."

And so it was for a long time. Some wise men wrote down the story of those voyages and of that land, and people read the tale and liked it, but no one remembered where the place was. It all seemed like a fairy tale. Long afterwards, however, men began to read those stories with wide-open eyes and to wonder. They guessed and talked together, and studied this and that land, and read the story over and over. At last they have learned that Wineland was in America, on the eastern shore of the United States, and they have called Snorri the first American, and have put up statues of Leif Ericsson, the first comer to America.[15]

---

15 See note about Eskimos on page 148.

House. In a rich Norseman's home were many buildings. The finest and largest was the great feast hall. Next were the bower, where the women worked, and the guest house, where visitors slept. Besides these were storehouses, stables, work-shops, a kitchen, a sleeping-house for thralls. All these buildings were made of heavy, hewn logs, covered with tar to fill the cracks and to keep the wood from rotting. The ends of the logs, the door-posts, the peaks of gables, were carved into shapes of men and animals and were painted with bright colors. These gay buildings were close together, often set around the four sides of a square yard. That yard was a busy and pleasant place, with men and women running across from one bright building to another. Sometimes a high fence with one gate went around all this, and only the tall, carved peaks of roofs showed from the outside.

Names. An old Norse story says: "Most men had two names in one, and thought it likeliest to lead to long life and good luck to have double names." To be called after a god was very lucky. Here are some of those double names with their meanings: "Thorstein" means Thor's stone; "Thorkel" means Thor's fire; "Thorbiorn" means Thor's bear; "Gudbrand" means Gunnr's sword (Gunnr was one of the Valkyrias[16]); "Gunnbiorn" means Gunnr's bear; "Gudrid" means Gunnr's rider; "Gudrod" means Gunnr's land-clearer. (Most of the land in old Norway was covered with forests. When a man got new land he had to clear off the trees.) In those olden days a man did not have a surname that belonged to everyone in his family. Sometimes there were two or three men of the same name in a neighborhood. That caused trouble. People thought of two ways of making it easy to tell which man was being spoken of. Each was given a nickname. Suppose the name

16 See note about Valkyrias on page 147.

of each was Haki. One would be called Haki the Black because he had black hair. The other would be called Haki the Ship-chested because his chest was broad and strong. These nicknames were often given only for the fun of it. Most men had them,–Eric the Red, Leif the Lucky, Harald Hairfair, Rolf Go-afoot. The other way of knowing one Haki from the other was to tell his father's name. One was Haki, Eric's son. The other was Haki, Halfdan's son. If you speak these names quickly, they sound like Haki Ericsson and Haki Halfdansson. After a while they were written like that, and men handed them on to their sons and daughters. Some names that we have nowadays have come down to us in just that way–Swanson, Anderson, Peterson, Jansen. There was another reason for these last names: a man was proud to have people know who his father was.

Drinking-horns. The Norsemen had few cups or goblets. They used instead the horns of cattle, polished and trimmed with gold or silver or bronze. They were often very beautiful, and a man was almost as proud of his drinking-horn as of his sword.

Tables. Before a meal thralls brought trestles into the feast hall and set them before the benches. Then they laid long boards across from trestle to trestle. These narrow tables stretched all along both sides of the hall. People sat at the outside edge only. So the thralls served from the middle of the. room. They put baskets of bread and wooden platters of meat upon these bare boards. At the end of the meal they carried out tables and all, and the drinking-horns went round in a clean room.

Beds. Around the sides of the feast hall were shut-beds. They were like big boxes with doors opening into the hall. On the floor of this box was straw with blankets thrown over it. The people got into these beds and closed the doors and so shut themselves in. Olaf's men could have set heavy things against these doors or have put props against them. Then the people could not have got out; for on the other side of the bed was the thick outside wall of the feast hall, and there were no windows in it.

Feast Hall. The feast hall was long and narrow, with a door at each end. Down the middle of the room were flat stones in the dirt floor. Here the fires burned. In the roof above these fires were holes for the smoke to go out, but some of it blew about the hall, and the walls and rafters were stained with it. But it was pleasant wood smoke, and the Norsemen did not dislike it. There were no large windows in a feast hall or in any other Norse building. High up under the eaves or in the roof itself were narrow slits that were called wind's-eyes. There was no glass in them, for the Norsemen did not know how to make it; but there were, instead, covers made of thin, oiled skin. These were put into the wind's-eyes in stormy weather. There were covers, too, for the smoke-holes. The only light came through these narrow holes, so on dark days the people needed the fire as much for light as for warmth.

Foster-father. A Norse father sent his children away from home to grow up. They went when they were three or four years old and stayed until they were grown. The father thought: "They will be better so. If they stayed at home, their mother would spoil them with much petting."

Foster-brothers. When two men loved each other very much they said, "Let us become foster-brothers."

Then they went and cut three long pieces of turf and put a spear into the ground so that it held up the strips of turf like an arch. Runes were cut on the handle of the spear, telling the duties of foster-brothers. The two men walked under this arch, and each made a little cut in his palm. They knelt and clasped hands, so that the blood of the two flowed together, and they said, "Now we are of one blood."

Then each made this vow: "I will fight for my foster-brother whenever he shall need me. If he is killed before I am, I will punish the man who did it. Whatever things I own are as much as my foster-brother's as mine. I will love this man until I die. I call Odin and Thor and all the gods to hear my vow. May they hate me if I break it!"

Ran. Ran was the wife of Aegir, who was god of the sea. They lived in a cave at the bottom of the ocean. Ran had a great net, and she caught in it all men who were shipwrecked and took them to her cave. She also caught all the gold and rich treasures that went down in ships. So her cave was filled with shining things.

Valkyrias. These were the maidens of Odin. They waited

on the table in Valhalla. But whenever a battle was being fought they rode through the air on their horses and watched to see what warriors were brave enough to go to Valhalla. Sometimes during the fight a man would think that he saw the Valkyrias. Then he was glad; for he knew that he would go to Valhalla.

An old Norse story says this about the Valkyrias: "With lightning around them, with bloody shirts of mail, and with shining spears they ride through the air and the ocean. When their horses shake their manes, dew falls on the deep valleys and hail on the high forests."

Odin's Ravens. Odin had a great throne in his palace in Asgard. When he sat in it he could look all over the world. But it was so far to see that he could not tell all of the things that were happening. So he had two ravens to help him. An old Norse story tells this about them: "Two ravens sit on Odin's shoulders and whisper in his ears all that they have heard and seen. He sends them out at dawn of day to see over the whole world. They return at evening near meal time. This is why Odin knows so many things."

Reykjavik. Reykjavik means "smoky sea." Ingolf called it that because of the steaming hot-springs by the sea. The place is still called Reykjavik. A little city has grown up there, the only city in Iceland. It is the capital of the country.

Peace-bands. A Norseman always carried his sword, even at a feast; for he did not know when he might need it. But when he went somewhere on an errand of peace and had no quarrel he tied his sword into its scabbard with white bands that he called peace-bands. If all at once something happened to make him need his sword, he broke the peace-bands and drew it out.

Eskimos. Now, the Eskimos live in Greenland and Alaska and on the very northern shores of Canada. But once they lived farther south in pleasanter lands. After a while the other Indian tribes began to grow strong. Then they wanted the pleasant land of the Eskimos and the seashore that the Eskimos had. So they fought again and again with those people and won and drove them farther north and farther north. At last the Eskimos were on the very shores of the cold sea, with the Indians still pushing them on. So some of them got into their boats and rowed across the narrow water and came to Greenland and lived there. Some people think that these things happened before Eric found Greenland. In that case he found Eskimos there; and Thorfinn saw red Indians in Wineland. Other people think that this happened after Eric went to Greenland. If that is true, he found an empty land, and it was Eskimos that Thorfinn saw in Wineland.

POSSIBLY this book seems made up of four or five disconnected stories. They are, however, strung upon one thread,–the westward emigration from Norway. The story of Harald is intended to serve in two ways towards the working out of this plot. It gives the general setting that continues throughout the book in costume, houses, ideals, habits. It explains the cause of the emigration from the mother country. It is really an introductory chapter. As for the other stories, they are distinctly steps in the progress of the plot. A chain of islands loosely connects Norway with America,–Orkneys and Shetlands, Faroes, Iceland, Greenland. It was from link to link of this chain that the Norsemen sailed in search of home and adventure. Discoveries were made by accident. Ships were driven by the wind from known island to unknown. These two points,–the island connection that made possible the long voyage from Norway to America, and the contribution of storm to discovery,–I have stated in the book only dramatically. I emphasize them here, hoping that the teacher will make sure that the children see them, and possibly that they state them abstractly.

Let me speak as to the proper imaging of the stories. I have not often interrupted incident with special description, not because I do not consider the getting of vivid and detailed images most necessary to full enjoyment and to proper intellectual habits, but because I trusted to the pictures of this book and to the teacher to do what seemed to me inartistic to do in the story. Some of these descriptions and explanations I have introduced into the book in the form of notes, hoping that the children in turning to them might form a habit of insisting upon full understanding of a point, and might possibly, with the teacher's encouragement, begin the habit of reference reading.

The landscape of Norway, Iceland, and Greenland is wonderful and will greatly assist in giving reality and definiteness to the stories. Materials for this study are not difficult of access. Foreign colored photographs of Norwegian landscape are becoming common in our art stores. There are good illustrations in the geographical works referred to in the book list. These could be copied upon the blackboard. There are three books beautifully illustrated in color that it will be possible to find only in large libraries,–"Coast of Norway," by Walton; "Travels in the Island of Iceland," by Mackenzie; "Voyage en Islande et au Gröenland," by J. P. Gaimard. If the landscape is studied from the point of view of formation, the images will be more accurate and more easily gained, and the study will have a general value that will continue past the reading of these stories into all work in geography.

Trustworthy pictures of Norse houses and costumes are difficult to obtain. In "Viking Age" and "Story of Norway," by Boyesen (G. P. Putnam's Sons, New York), are many copies of Norse antiquities in the fashion of weapons, shield-bosses, coins, jewelry, wood-carving. These are, of course, accurate, but of little interest to children. Their chief value lies in helping the teacher to piece together a picture that she can finally give to her pupils.

Metal-working and wood-carving were the most important arts of the Norse. If children study products of these arts and actually do some of the work, they will gain a quickened sympathy with the people and an appreciation of their power. They may, perhaps, make something to merely illustrate Norse work; for instance, a carved ship's-head, or a copper shield, or a wrought door-nail. But, better, they may apply Norse ideas of form and decoration and Norse processes in making some modern thing that they can actually use; for instance, a carved wood pin-tray or a copper match holder. This work should lead out into a study of these same industries among ourselves with visits to wood-working shops and metal foundries.

Frequent drawn or painted illustration by the children

of costumes, landscapes, houses, feast halls, and ships will help to make these images clear. But dramatization will do more than anything else for the interpreting of the stories and the characters. It would be an excellent thing if at last, through the dramatization and the handwork, the children should come to sufficient understanding and enthusiasm to turn skalds and compose songs in the Norse manner. This requires only a small vocabulary and a rough feeling for simple rhythm, but an intensity of emotion and a great vividness of image.

These Norse stories have, to my thinking, three values. The men, with the crude courage and the strange adventures that make a man interesting to children, have at the same time the love of truth, the hardy endurance, the faithfulness to plighted word, that make them a child's fit companions. Again, in form and in matter old Norse literature is well worth our reading. I should deem it a great thing accomplished if the children who read these stories should so be tempted after a while to read those fine old books, to enjoy the tales, to appreciate straightforwardness and simplicity of style. The historical value of the story of Leif Ericsson and the others seems to me to be not to learn the fact that Norsemen discovered America before Columbus did, but to gain a conception of the conditions of early navigation, of the length of the voyage, of the dangers of the sea, and a consequent realization of the reason for the fact that America was unknown to mediæval Europe, of why the Norsemen did not travel, of what was necessary to be done before men should strike out across the ocean. Norse story is only one chapter in that tale of American discovery. I give below an outline of a year's work on the subject that was once followed by the fourth grade of the Chicago Normal School. The idea in it is to give importance, sequence, reasonableness, broad connections, to the discovery of America.

The head of the history department who planned this course says it is "in a sense a dramatization of the development of geographical knowledge."

Following is a bare topical outline of the work:

- Evolution of the forms of boats.
- Viking Tales.
- A crusade as a tale of travel and discovery.
- Monasteries as centers of work.
- Printing.
- Story of Marco Polo.
- Columbus' discovery.
- Story of Vasco da Gama.
- Story of Magellan.

A Pronouncing Index

(This index and guide to pronunciation which are given to indicate the pronunciation of the more difficult words, are based upon the 1918 edition of Webster's New International Dictionary.)

Aegir (ē' jĭr)
Ȧrā' bĭ *a*
Ärn' vĭd
Ăs' gärd
Aud' bĭ ôrn
Ạu' dŭn

Bĭ är' nĭ

Eric (ē' rĭk)
Ericsson (ĕr' ĭk sŭn)
Eyjolf (ī' yôlf)

Faroes (fā' rōz)
fiord (fyôrd)
Flō' kĭ

Grĭm
Gŭd' bränd
Gŭd' rĭd
Gŭd' rōd
Gŭn*n*' bĭ ôrn
Gụ' t*h*ôrm
Gyda (gē' dȧ)

Hä' kĭ
Hä' kôn
Hälf' dăn
Hăr' ăld
Hä' värd
Hĕl' ä
Hĕl' gȧ
Hẽr' st*e*īn
Holmstein (hōlm' stīn)

Ĭn' gôlf
Ī' vär

Leif (līf)

Niflheim (nĕv' 'l hām)

Ō' dĭn
Ō' läf
Orkneys (ôrk' nĭz)

Rän
Reykjavík (rā' ky*ȧ* vēk')
Rôlf

Shĕt' l*ă*nds
Sif (sēf)
Sighvat (sĭg' vät)
Snorri (snŏr' rē)
Sôl' fĭ

Thor (thôr)
T*h*ôr' bĭ ôrn
T*h*ôr' fĭnn
T*h*ôr' gĕst
T*h*ôr' hĭld
T*h*ôr' kĕl
T*h*ôr' l*e*īf
T*h*ôr' ôlf
T*h*ôr' st*e*īn
Tyrker (tẽr' kẽr)

Văl häl' l*ȧ*
Valkyria (văl kĭr' y*ȧ*)
Vī' kĭng

A GUIDE TO PRONUNCIATION

ā	as in **āle**	ē	as in **ēve**	ō	as in **ōbey'**
ă	as in **ădd**	ê	as in **ê vent'**	ŏ	as in **ŏdd**
ă	as in **find*ă*l**	ĕ	as in **ĕnd**	ô	as in **lôrd**
ȧ	as in **ȧsk**	ẽ	as in **hẽr**	ŭ	as in **ŭp**
ȧ	as in **sof*ȧ***	ī	as in **īce**	*ŭ*	as in **circ*ŭ*s**
ä	as in **ärm**	ĭ	as in **ĭt**	ụ	as in **rụde**
ạ	as in **ạll**	ō	as in **ōld**	ȳ	as in **flȳ**

Silent letters are italicized.